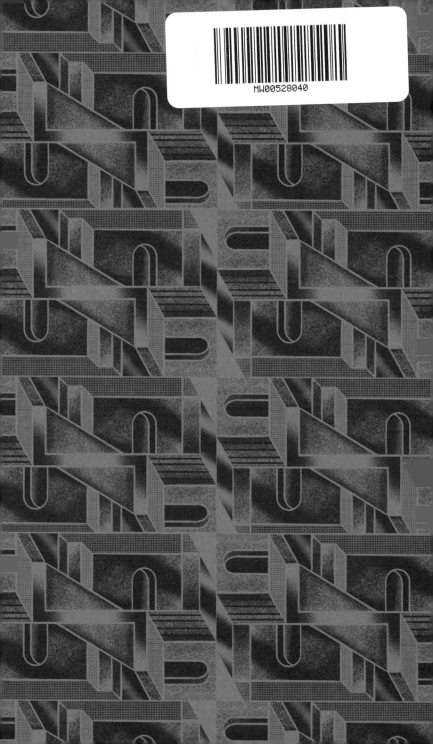

MW00528040

COUP de GRÂCE

SOFIA AJRAM

TITAN BOOKS

Coup de Grâce
Hardback edition ISBN: 9781803369624
E-book edition ISBN: 9781803369631

Published by Titan Books
A division of Titan Publishing Group Ltd.
144 Southwark Street, London SE1 0UP
www.titanbooks.com

First edition: October 2024
10 9 8 7 6 5 4 3 2

This is a work of fiction. All of the characters, organizations,
and events portrayed in this novel are either products of the author's
imagination or are used fictitiously. Any resemblance to actual persons,
living or dead (except for satirical purposes), is entirely coincidental.

© Sofia Ajram 2024

Sofia Ajram asserts the moral right to be identified as the author of this work.

A CIP catalogue record for this title is available from the British Library.

Printed and bound by CPI (UK) Ltd, Croydon, CR0 4YY

AUTHOR'S NOTE

Coup de Grâce is a story primarily about depression and suicide. In dealing with these subjects, the book includes scenes with reference to suicidal ideation and depictions of self-harm.

If you or someone you know is contemplating suicide, please reach out for support. Please do not struggle in silence.

For those who understand.

Can we try it another way?

— JUSTIN BENSON & AARON MOORHEAD, *Resolution*

I HAVE SOME SAD NEWS for you. I've condemned myself to die. I try to treat this with as much eloquence and compassion as a work of art. It is, of course, the most important thing any of us may ever say, so I will paint it with the melancholy of a poet. Psyche, not awakened by the light touch of an arrow, but a kiss. A kiss with the waves.

I've decided that's how, and the time is now.

All I can think about, as the subway rushes to lift me there, is a story I read somewhere about a man who walked into the North Sea. When they finally recovered his bloated white body, belly full of rocks, there was an unused train ticket in his pocket. A return ticket to London. He must've held the choice until the very end.

I'M GOING, GOING, GONE.

"You good, man?"

I slide a headphone off to hear. The air surges in, laps icy flumes around me. He sits down on the seat next to me, his hand brushing against my thigh. The subway chimes and the doors close. Odd place to cruise, but stranger things have happened.

"Yeah, you?"

"Sure," he says. Shifts in his seat.

Across from us, there's an ad for the Montreal Museum of Fine Arts' exhibition on taboo in art. *Don't Look Back* is plastered across every poster in bubblegum pink. Along the seats, cresting the sliding doors of the Metro, are image reproductions of various myths: Orpheus looking back upon Eurydice, Psyche beholding Eros, men casting their eyes upon Medusa—all with dire consequence.

The one nearest us is Lot's wife of the Book of Genesis looking back upon the destruction of Sodom, dissolved to a pillar of salt—an ill portent.

He asks me if I've seen the show. I haven't.

"Have you?"

"Yeah," he says.

I look at him. Knowing this'll be the last person I talk to before I die.

A soft mess of curls, the colour of earth. Gloves tucked into his pockets, hunched over, glasses dangling from his fingers as though to indicate some sort of softness. He is so beautiful. Very handsome, so it all makes sense. I like him at once, overwhelmingly. There is a confidence that comes with the ease of loveliness. Not many are on the train, but everyone is looking at him, his freckled, sun-kissed skin. I want to pour into his lap.

I pick at a sticker on the shiny plastic subway bench as he talks to me about the exhibit. His voice is pleasant. The sticker depicts an angry little demon cherub, cherry-red cheeks and cherry-red horns, chin resting into a plump little fist under a curved banner that reads *No terfs no swerfs no fascists!* Across the back of the seat are the words *YUPPIE SCUM* scratched in with crosshatched lines like an inmate counting days of solitary.

The doors open on Charlevoix station. A bridge bisects the subway rails, like Radisson, where a woman jumped onto the tracks last month. I'd plunged in after her, equipped with a critical care kit and a guilty impotence, murmuring prayers and platitudes as we scraped her broken body off the concrete. When you can't afford school past pre-med, you either sign up to be a combat medic or become an EMT. Serve the community or serve the nation; I'll let you guess which one I picked.

Some claim it's easy (but then, of course, they wouldn't be here if it were). Wherever you turn your gaze, strategies to end it all are evergreen: every sheer rock cliff and briny river bend; freedom hanging from every branch of every twisted, barren tree. Every plastic bag and pill and vein: a tool, a weapon—a means to set you free. Each and every one of these possibilities is a temporary stanch on a suicide's journey: station after station, like a subway stopping momentarily on its way to a terminus. There's no deluding yourself into disembarking or changing direction. I can't be a jumper—on the tracks, from a rooftop, a bridge—I'm just not built for it. I've tried other approaches. There've been so many. My choice is slated. Inked in blood, it grips me.

I've been battling depression and anxiety disorders since I was an adolescent. Lately it's gotten worse. You'd think that I'd have my shit under control, but this stage between youth and middle age is where life hits you with a series of premature bereavements. The withering ember of dreams. Finances. Aging parents. The future. We are promised the world, but by the time we hit thirty, life knocks us over the head with a baseball bat like we're a fucking piñata at a gender reveal party and we're struck by the futility of it all: our finances are indelibly fucked, our dreams are scattered ash and the future has been salted.

Yet, despite all that, I sometimes relapse into hope. Just as Orpheus, just as Lot's wife, at times I turn, as a result of sudden, mad temptation for the lust of life, of love, of remembering, and look back upon living with fondness, and embrace uncertainty.

Heavy, the coat of habit that one drapes atop the shoulders of life.

Peel station, and the doors shudder closed. The subway is mostly vacant. I swap my attention to the stranger beside me.

"Where are you heading?" he says.

Away, for good.

"The beach," I tell him.

"Montreal has a beach?"

"Sort of."

It does, but it's not the one you're thinking of.

The closest body of water is the Saint Lawrence River, which travels south to Lake Ontario, and extends north-east into the Gulf of Saint Lawrence, and the Atlantic at large.

Not the picturesque and brutal North Sea, but neither was the River Seine, the Tamagawa Canal, or, in the case of Virginia Woolf, who filled her overcoat pockets with stones, the River Ouse near Lewes.

I had chosen this as my River Ouse. I will ride to the terminus, then disembark and walk east until I yield myself to the riverbank and break like a summer heat against the Saint Lawrence, devoured and swept away.

My life has been incredibly good, I have people in it and happiness, and some days I feel resolute, but let's be honest: if at its best it's not enough, then what can save me?

At Berri-UQAM station, the stranger stands and turns to me momentarily so I can glimpse his expression painted with that Dionysian impulse I know all too well. Then he disem-barks. I follow him out and up the steps, trying not to think for a second.

By the exit butterfly doors, the lumpy silhouette of a man, knees drawn, dozes on a bench. A weathered arm, bruised and battered, dangles out from beneath his coat, fingertips nearly grazing the tile. I've been called to one too many scenes with someone sporting those bruises, just to take them away in an ambulance. If I were staying around in this world, maybe I'd see him next week.

We stride past him in silence.

There's a public washroom just outside the station. The doors unlock after fifteen minutes are up, but that's all the time we need.

By reflex of omission, I do not let him touch me. Being naked deranges me. Even like this, near the end, I cannot grant anyone the gentle, unconscious grace of taming my body, of warming it with pleasure. It is a poison, a stigmata I fear enough to spare others the contagion of. But I do break the fast with his lips, allowing small and subtle touches. I wonder if he can read death in my eyes. I look in the mirror and try to see if anything has changed. The choice that's been made. Can people see it in me?

When we're done, he gives his name. Felix.

"I'm Vicken," I say.

He smiles.

What are you thinking?

I'm thinking I want to ask for more than just his name. The urge emboldens me, like a mouse daring to dash around a venomous snake, though I stifle it down. It's hard to be so close to something just out of reach.

We go back to the Metro and cross an image of Psyche discovering the darkly sleeping Cupid, and sit once more across from Lot's wife. *This again*, I think. The rising flames. Angels casting fire and brimstone. I want to white myself out of Sodom's apocalypse and chisel it instead into the arms of Aphrodite's son, Eros.

A couple stations pass in silence.

"Why'd they keep looking back if they knew the gods would punish them for it?" Felix nudges his chin at the poster.

I shrug. So very many theories. "Grief; a last taste of life," I say. I suppose Lot's wife was reluctant to tear herself away from the world she would leave behind.

"Grief?"

"If we don't live in the present, we lose the very thing we're trying to seize."

"*Philosophical*," he says, and his eyes go wide.

"Shut up," I say, and again, he smiles wryly.

We sit in silence and it feels almost… comfortable. But I find that when I think about it, there's a lot of moments like this, that feel briefly perfect, where my soul quivers. We're constantly deceived by the largeness of life on movie screens, in literature. Overwhelming and fond memories of strangers, failed heavens. Slipping by someone in the street, meeting their eyes. Shyly looking askant.

It does make me want to jostle that metaphorical Magic 8 Ball, see what other answers might be divined from that blue haze.

Should I be doing this?

Shake-shake.

Yes.

Can I wait another day?

Shake-shake.

Concentrate and ask again.

I wet my lips. For a shocking moment, deliciously proud, I'm thinking of a million different verbal offerings, flirtations that might dock me at the station of love and not that of oblivion. I could turn this thing right around. A chance meeting could change my life. Maybe. *Fuck it*, I think. If he says no, I'll never see this guy again, and anyway, this is my big day, baby. Big as a battering ram, trying to feel just as big; toothy grin, in case I fumble. Can't let anyone ruin this moment. And no one can ruin it for me. Because there's no one else on the Metro.

But, the moment I turn to ask, my lips forming the words I've rehearsed in my mind during the passage of the last two stations: *want to see that show again, sometime—with me?*, someone walks in and sits near us and suddenly, the exile of desire strobes inside me like a thunderclap. My wave of narcissism evaporates under the stranger's wolf-gaze and I sit there, mutely.

Shake-shake.

My reply is no.

I feel like the nominee who, having the audacity to believe he might win, holds blissful unawareness, reacting blithely to all that shines on him the banquet evening, and, subsequently, is cast out of heaven by his loss. It is what it was always going to be. A kiss with the cold black-blue waves of the Saint Lawrence River.

Just as I think this, he gets up to leave. The Metro slows and the doors open upon Assomption station.

"Well," he says. "See you."

"See you," I say.

It is what it is. It's hard to talk when you're depressed. The words carve intaglio calligraphy, wrap around your neck like a noose. Lord knows that's not the only place. Other times, I write the pain on my limbs, opening words in sporadic mutilation across my skin. If Felix does remember me—remember that I existed—it'll only be that I sucked him off in a restroom.

He stands at the threshold. I see him hesitate a moment.

Digging into his pocket, he pulls out a glossy white transport ticket and a marker. He uncaps the marker with his teeth and keeps it cornered between his lips as he bends down. Scrawls something illegible from my vantage point, then steps back two paces and hands it to me. Caps the pen.

I knit my brows.

Felix, it says. And then a phone number.

There is silence for a moment, followed immediately by that little three-note chime. The Société de transport de Montréal's signature music-box jingle, the off-key overture of "Lucy in the Sky With Diamonds" that signals the departure of a train. And before I have a chance to protest—to process, even—what is going on, the doors slide closed. The engine thrums with tension and then chokes to life. Felix is on the other side of the doors, grinning, then vanishes.

I turn inward, away from the stranger looking at me and I pocket the ticket with his number on it. I don't know why. Nobody can save anybody.

Well. All right, I think to myself. *This is it, my little bug.* Big day ahead. Think I will cozy up and try to get some sleep before I do this. Eyes on the prize. If I overthink it, I might change my mind. Sometimes I love this world too much. To the moon and back, really. Forever.

I put my headphones on and dial up my voicemail. I've got one from last week. I've been trying to understand what the voice is saying before my cell plan wipes it. I listen to it on loop. Like ASMR, it comforts me. Pitiful silence between snatches of words that make up a phrase. I can barely hear them, but the voice sounds just like my own, dark and drowsy. Words of affirmation—so noble. My love language.

Sweet dreams, I tell it. I hope we'll go someplace safe.

I T STARTS AS A pinprick needle point, face-on; microscopic.
A luminous dot. Unfolding itself from behind, wiggling from dot to line—a thread—dancing in an ocean of darkness. The sky before the stars, it is a growing skein of constellations, bleak and unrecognizable. Their essence starts to fade and at once explodes in a fit of fury into a thousand shards, wriggles and broils, effervescing into something larger and more complex; impaling slats of light, a howl of fluorescence through darkness no longer shrouded in emptiness, but gestating, somehow, into an empty room; room; *rooms*,

multiplying like cells; mapping the interior void from which we later arise.

Escalators shudder out like a sigh. Lights shiver, flicker to life. Cement runs like a river, down walls and crashes against stairwells—wide and narrow—clipping off into geometries that evaporate into corners. Openings and doorways refract, kaleidoscopic, and telescope infinitely upon themselves in unfolding duplicates. Platforms open onto wide-open chasms, cement gorges like waterless dams, and this becomes a place of dis-ease—the familiar emptiness of underground parking lots, hotel conference rooms after hours, or defunct play structures for children.

The atmosphere is smoky grey. Dark. Penumbra almost-dusk, but stripped of any colour. Seemingly small, it unravels into a boundless labyrinth with no way out but through, though the path is not known and sometimes the scale of it is immense, a maddening canvas of toyed perspectives, and I cannot imagine the power that builds this, the hand that paints the walls heavy with concrete.

When I get here, which I inevitably will—most of us do, though we'll never see but glimpses of each other, some suspended for impossibly long braids of time—I'll be determined to explore as much as I can. After all, it was made for me. And I'll be here until I prevail or at least until I can no longer stand it.

After that, I pray I be kind.

TERMINUS. MERCI D'AVOIR VOYAGÉ avec la STM.
Bonne journée.

WHERE MY FEET STEP off, groggy and mired in confusion, there are no station plaques, which is funny, because that's not a place that exists, like some twisted Black Lodge or LesterCorp Floor 7 ½, and while I'm thinking about these things and the wry humour of them, the subway chimes, the doors behind me glide shut, and, with a puff of air, like a rising gale, the train plunges down the track into the black maw and vanishes into the void.

When I spin around to face the tracks, they are empty. A thick yellow stripe lines the length of the platform, denoting the edge. There is a trench where the tracks lie, though no visible outbound tracks that I can see. A few stations are like this in Montreal, namely De l'Église and Charlevoix—the deepest station in the network— where platforms are constructed with narrow access points folded one on top of the other rather than side-by-side. There is no natural illumination, only the incandescent glow of fluorescent lights crawling along the platform overhead like a millipede. The smell is that of old buildings: wet concrete, dark and damp and dense; the sound of it, the whispered mono-frequency of aircraft white noise, of liminal thresholds between continents.

I look sidelong down the platform. It is empty.

I glance at my phone. No missed calls, no texts. No bars. It's late, and I can see that I've overslept; wasted precious time. I creep onward and bound up the stairs at the end of the platform in twos. There's only about thirteen steps, and then a short landing that rotates and leads to a second set. At the summit is a floor-to-ceiling turnstile gate, similar in operation to a one-way revolving door, but with metal teeth, eliminating the possibility of re-entry. The permission only to exit and not re-enter the platform gives me hesitation. I don't know where I am but I'm pretty confident that all I have to do is go around and find the opposite platform, and so I push through.

On the other side is a battlement overseeing the platform below, and I think to myself, *Must be some new extension in Sherbrooke, east past the Saint Lawrence—*

But as I come up, I'm greeted with the bulge of polished metal, more nauseating amounts of grey and another hallway, like a maintenance tunnel, that funnels into a ripple of stairs up to more and more grey.

When I emerge into the next atrium, face flushed, I can hardly breathe. My pace scatters along but then stops as the foretaste of dread hits me with prodigious force. It seems at once impossible to claim that it's only my imagination.

There is no outbound platform.

An astonishing bewilderment fills me, then patinas with frustration. What's extra-fucking-ass is that this is cutting in on my plans. I hadn't scheduled an excursion to concrete wonderland, and the more time that ticks by, the further in the day we get, and then rush hour, the arteries of Montreal's subway line pulsing with life, and the fervour of it might get me to change my mind; it has before, so I'm trying to hurry it up, the way you hurry up and schedule a dentist appointment first thing in the morning—to get it over with.

I hurry down another hall, thinking, this time, for sure: the outbound platform. But no. At the end is something else entirely.

At first, I don't see the necessity for such complex geometry. It seems to violate the laws of physics and bend the laws of nature.

It is insurmountably large, a gargantuan organ that possesses the verticality of a tower. Every bit of it seems made of concrete, that subtle wash of slate-grey, dark and sovereign. There are snapshots of other material, the cut of stainless-steel banisters, gently wafting empty escalators sweeping up three stories past the point of converging lines telescoping in on themselves before disappearing, acrylic sheets covering tiled ads for a Thai food restaurant: two bobble-headed faces with chattering marionette teeth and too-white eyes girdling an Oktoberfest special, their faces not quite right, as though processed ineffectively by some artificial mechanism. There is a row of eight STM-branded turnstiles, and an empty control kiosk emanating a jaundiced bioluminescence. The light is of a place once visited—in a dream, as a child. To me, it is wildly disorienting.

Protrusions and overhangs make it impossible to see around certain edges, hiding things in shadows, openings perhaps, doorways and crawl spaces, and as I step forward, I find myself questioning: just how much of it is accessible? How much of it is decorative?

There is stillness here, though not in the way that a church is still, or a meadow, or a shore. It is a place that has intention— an interior built for humans, wholly unoccupied by them. A place that has been here a long time. Big, with function, for people, but devoid of any life and imbuing the space with a mild perception of wrongness.

It gradually dawns on me that I've been denied a destination, caught in a transitional environment, a space between beginning and an end. What I see towers benedictive above my head, and is certainly not Honoré-Beaugrand terminus; I know this now.

Here stands a structure whose purpose was made for people. A space with a very clear intention. Deserted. For-gotten. It's weird, I think. I don't know. A space made for travelers, void of such motion, and I cannot dispose of its perverse emptiness.

I'm dwarfed by the scale of it.

Every bit of it is carved into rough, angular lines. There are no curves, save for the semi-circular handrail gently churning over the newels of the escalators at their landing thresholds. Few of the ceilings are flat. They soar up, forty, fifty feet and cut at odd facets, sometimes meeting in neat triangles, other times disseminating into geometries that make no sense.

Fluorescent lights flood from everywhere, emanating a faint buzz, but still the place seems dark as though oneiric: a disturbing cast of greenish colour-temperature diffused through protruding beams and slanted balconies, their grooved ceiling lines, as though fingers dragged through the sand, but no, there is nothing natural about this place.

This subway station, like any city structure, is a space entirely constructed by humans. Even city parks, gardens, and manufactured waterways, which seem to us wild and natural, have been girdled and domesticated by the hands of urban planning. The unpainted concrete, the entirely exposed interior, a vivisection of a body, peeled open like a fruit, its anatomy set on display—I've never seen anything like it. Brutalism is so utilitarian, so institutional. It moves directly against nostalgia. So how is this place then so nostalgic? Why is it both so familiar and so alien? And from where does this nostalgia arise for a place I've never been?

Therein lies the incongruity. There is something dissonant about this place, and it's more than just the look of it. It's the sense that this space was deliberately created to guide busy lives through its arteries and ventricles—passageways for passengers— and in this moment, they are empty. Just for me.

LATER—MUCH LATER, EVEN—I still haven't seen a single exit.
My phone is of no use. No signal. I key in a slew of text messages to my mom, all of which fail to send. I consider sending one to Felix, then think better of it.

I'm staring through the metal spokes of the multi-arm turnstiles like a prisoner, no subways ever appearing at the platform, when a voice startles me from behind.

"Of course it coughs up a train the second I leave."

I spin around like a cornered animal. Facing me is a woman with frail, milk-glass bone structure. Her nebulous and uneven grey hair descends in matted plaits. She is ensconced in a pashmina scarf. It gathers in swathes of damask and paisley mulberry print, overly baroque and threadbare like the patterned wings of a moth draped over her shoulders, which dwarfs her even further. She resembles something drowned: her skin pale and colourless, vascular-marbled; her eyes watery and dull, lit by only a spark of irritation. And she's carrying that same empty look about her I know too well.

As she approaches me, I back myself against the metal turnstile.

"Calm down," she says. "What's your name?"

"Vick," I say.

"Vick," she repeats. "How long have you been here?"

"Um. I have no idea. Where is 'here' exactly?"

She ignores this. "Which way did you come?"

"What do you mean?"

"I mean: how did you get here?"

"From the Metro. What's going on?"

"When?"

Her blaze of questions is starting to freak me out. "I don't know—an hour, two?"

Her scowl stretches. "Do you have a phone?"

I fumble with it and she snatches it from my palm.

She gestures to it. "You have a charger for this?"

When I shake my head she stomps away in a hairpin loop: off, then back around. Her walk is a staggered *thu-thud*, like a heartbeat. It doesn't slow her pace, but it makes her look like a canted tree when she leans her body weight onto her left side. Makes me think she's got signs of rot and necrosis somewhere under her clothing where I can't see, down in her roots.

"There's no outbound platform in this station?" I ask, as she's holding my phone up comically to catch a signal. No reception. I tried. Sincerely. Even from the heights of the escalator. No dice.

"I do not have the energy for this today." She throws me a deadpan look. "No."

"I'm completely lost. How is that possible?"

"You're as sharp as a bowling ball," she snaps, dropping her arm that holds the phone. "I don't *know*, okay? I've been here two straight days and unless I backtrack to this stupid room I never see the same place twice. Stop jamming questions down my throat. I don't know."

I stand there and rub at my temples, feeling homesick for my thwarted day's plans. This is not how I wanted my afternoon to go. I'd be better off on my own—find an out, then make my way back to the Saint Lawrence River one way or another. Can't be that far.

"Okay… I'm just—" I point my finger guns off somewhere to the left of her. "I'm gonna go. Could you give me my phone back? *Please*," I add, when she gives me a sour look.

"*Go?*" she says. Her lips curl and she glares at me with this wide-eyed incredulous expression like she's just seen she's got shit on her shoe. Her brows crease together, then she drops the phone in my open palm, heavily. "I mean. Have fun, I guess? Leave some breadcrumbs behind you or something. But I can tell you from looking around there's not much off that way. If you need me, I'll be having a nice ugly cry lying down on the floor."

I watch her guiltily.

I don't know what else to do here. There's no clear path and I'm scared as hell.

Pashmina looks at me with bloodshot, hollow eyes. Her shoulders are shuddering. Inside me, something rises and crashes against my rib cage like a wave.

I think of every quit screen I've ever seen. *If you close this dialogue, anything not saved will be lost. Are you sure you wish to close?*

Well?

I find myself wondering, finally, with disconsolate gloom, if what I really want right now is to be alone.

"Actually," I say. My voice sounds like a void space. "Would you mind if I stay?"

WEDNESDAY. THURSDAY. FRIDAY. THESE days drift by like melodies. Initially I'm relieved to have someone else stuck in here with me, but Pashmina's a bit of a miserablist. That's obviously not her real name. I made a mistake in not asking her for it—didn't think we'd be here together for this long, and now we're so past the "nice to meet you" stage that I can't even lightly self-deprecate my way into asking what it is. What would you want me to do? Ask her to role-play as strangers meeting for the first time? I'm Vicken, and you are? A dickhead or just dumb? Don't answer that.

Most suicidal people I've met are pretty sardonic. Whatever helps the medicine go down, I guess, but that never goes over well with shrinks or chronic killjoys. It's not in vogue to have that Virginia Woolf thing going on anymore. That just pisses people off. At least Virginia Woolf had something to write home about. Her journal is rife with trauma and tragedy. I'm just like a teen boy stuck in a perpetual hormonal state of despair. I've been living like this for as long as I can remember. No trigger; just clinically headfucked. Imagine having a perennial case of boss music, and you'd feel some ways about it, too.

She doesn't want to talk to me, but we're scared of losing sight of each other, so I follow her around like a stray. At first I was atrociously afraid of her but nothing bonds people together quite like trauma.

We've decided on a place to eat and a place to shit and a place to cry. Rooms upon rooms, unreaming like silk scarves from a magic hat. Last night, no alcohol to soothe me, I sought out a lonesome place like an animal, creeping into the opposite corner of the room from Pashmina. No mirror with which to see, no basin with which to cool my face. Simply: tears in a room, lit the same as all the others (no animal darkness either, then), just to come back, sniffling, and have Pashmina gaze at me with an indifferent, blunt face, then turn in disgust. She reads a book and drinks Cherry Coke. I get the sense she doesn't want me around but I'm unable to part ways from her.

Initially, I thought, *I'll run out of food and then that'll be the end of that. See! I'm a glass half-full kinda guy. An optimist at heart.* But then today we found a *dépanneur*—those concession-style convenience stores tucked at the corner of almost every bustling city street—along one of the doorless halls, contemporary glass and metal just sitting there jutting out of the wall, plain as day, and I feel like my bingo card of fuckery has filled every block. I have no idea what to believe I'll find in here anymore. You could park a Costco in one of these rooms and I'd just nod along once I found it, like, *Uh-huh. Okay, sure. Of course.*

Anyway, the good thing about the *dép* food is that I can eat the same thing repeatedly. I just hyper-fixate on one thing that tastes bland enough that I can stomach it, and eat that and only that for days or weeks or months until I literally can't stand it anymore. Jell-O cups and cheese sticks until I want to hurl.

We figure we should explore before my phone runs out of battery, depriving us of a flashlight, but this place never goes dark. There's a perpetual state of illumination flooding every inch of it, making sleep difficult and dream impossible.

I feel like we're in different stages of grief. She: in anger; myself: denial. The terrible truth is, I still can't explain what exactly is happening. I am lucid. I am awake. The day of Felix and my planned suicide, not so far away, is fading like a dream, and I cradle the broken fragments like they're the last bastion of my sanity. I can't bridge the gap between the station he disembarked at and where I am now, so I occupy the space in my mind with what grounds me in reality: my body. Every waking minute, we are moving. Passageways of roughened concrete undulate in and out of my vision, unbroken by ads or art or places to sit. The deeper we go, the less visual variety there is. Not that it matters. Pashmina's movements have a rushed sense of urgency about them, like she's running out of time, or like she's seen something I haven't: the peeled-back teeth of a bear trap poised to snap on the meat of our legs or some dreadful pair of eyes to this architectural beast, and I'm scared to ask what exactly she may have seen before I got here.

We're at the top of a flight of stairs, overlooking the volume of the station when she sets off for another enfilade. We've been walking for hours, barely without a break, and she already wants back at it. She picks up my cell phone and shines the flashlight at me. It flares across my eye, Archimedes' mirror. I wince away.

"Fuck this shit." She glares. "I don't want to be here."

This feels like an offhand remark on me as well, but by the time this registers, she's already striding halfway down the hall in her half-limp and I'm trotting up behind her like a dog again. We pass through corridors of discoloured ugly limewash concrete that look like they've sat for years, decades, millennia, untouched by human hand.

Pashmina keeps her head down, eyes trained to her footfalls, for sanity, grounding. One foot in front of the other, like she's in military basic.

The brutalist hallways continue, seemingly infinite angular corridors of storm-grey brick and mortar, until forty-five minutes later, up through an escalator that opens to a balcony clearing over twenty feet onto a platform, there is a maintenance tunnel-like hall that darkens, seems to soak in its converging lines, as if a contracting pupil. The ceiling is shorter here, seven or eight feet. The lights seem dimmer as well, the air thicker, somehow, like there is the presence of some immovable, unknowable thing buried in hunger up ahead.

"It's louder," Pashmina says to me conversationally. We are standing at the doorless threshold.

"What?"

"The noise." She hums a little and sweeps the flashlight of my phone around the space, illuminating more gunmetal and nauseating amounts of grey the colour of granite dust. She is right. There is a sound.

I don't understand how anything can make that chord—human or mechanical. It is too discordant, too big, to conceive of its orchestra.

"Where is it coming from?"

Down the hall, we'd imagine, but it's hard to decipher its orientation. Turning my head, it seems to evade me in an entirely new direction every time I pivot.

"It's gotta be tinnitus from pressure," I conclude. "We're probably hundreds of feet underground."

We traverse the darkened corridor, Pashmina at the vanguard with her finger trigger-ready on the camera to record, and we brace ourselves at every juncture to use it, to wince at the incredible sight of some Cold War-era experiment eroded into a hungry, wet mire, screeching octaves beyond what any human vocal cords could produce.

When we reach what looks to be the end of the hallway, we release a collective breath. Unornamented bedrock-grey concrete walls. No doors or alcoves or signs of fixtures of any kind. There's exactly nothing here.

"Fuck," she mutters.

"What now?"

We discuss potential plans. Pashmina is gliding her hand along the wall, hard and cold as rain.

"You skip a shower? It smells nasty," she remarks. And it does.

We sniff at the air, cats tasting the atmosphere. It's a crisp overture of ozone, that tinge of sterile cleaning agent, but underneath it is a rotten cocktail, ammonia-sour. Like the sickly husk of something trapped in an air vent.

An old boyfriend had shown me a video once where scientists had developed a lampricide based on the scent of dead sea lampreys. When the scent was poured into a tank of live ones, their panic response was so violent they damn nearly sprang out of the tank in pursuit of escape. I wonder for a second if this is what it smelled like.

"Oh, goodie," she says. She's looking over my shoulder at something behind me.

I turn and face the east wall.

"What the fuck?" I stiffen.

Before this room it makes sense. It's not dangerous. Darkness is only darkness, metal on masonry, a place buried or forgotten, somehow. House lights on in a haunted house. Up until now, there has been a healthy trepidation in response to the liminality of this place—an interior made for people, by people, completely void of a single soul.

So when we reach the end of this final corridor and find that to our right, a wall of concrete has unseamed, a horrible dread unfolds.

The tunnel is too dark, too deep to see into, even as Pashmina shoves my phone flashlight in. It's the height of the wall, around twelve feet, but only about a foot wide. I don't like this.

Oh, God. I reel. The smell is stronger now. It's coming from inside. Fumes of bitter tonalities, like a pungent and ascetic leathery marinade…

"It's like trying to find the plug behind my dresser. I can't see shit," she mutters and lowers the flashlight, covering her nose and mouth with her scarf.

We exchange glances. She gestures to the slat in the wall.

"Okay, pucker nuts."

"Wait," I say. "Hang on."

Such slipshod preparations for what's to come, and by that, I mean none. How much do I find myself trusting Pashmina's instinct? Can't we think about this a minute before we go urban spelunking in the God-size glory hole?

Her lips peel back, revealing the pointed edge of a tooth. "What other option do we have?"

"There's tons of rooms back there we haven't even seen yet."

Pashmina looks at me like the idea is preposterous, her vindicating eyes tracking up and down my body, as though exhausted by my idiocy. She starts mumbling to herself, the half-life of problem-solving, aged like milk. "What, exactly, are you hoping to find? A shortcut? We can just turn around if it's a dead end." An exasperation mounts in her eyes, adamantine. "If there's something in there, I want to get to it before it gets to us."

"'*Before it gets us*'? Before *what* gets us?"

"I don't know. Use your imagination! Screw it. I'm going in. What else are we gonna do? Nap—? Cry—?"

We've been doing just that and it hasn't been such a crapshoot, but Pashmina doesn't seem to give a shit. She's a woman at the end of her patience.

And, I suppose, trepidation or not, what do I care? What is it I'm avoiding? It's the kind of situation that begs mockery. Just another self-deception, knowing where I'm headed to begin with. Lest we forget.

Pashmina is whip-thin and slides along the smooth opening with ease. It's just broad enough to slip through, like snaking into a distended vertical wound in the wall.

I, already too big for most things—the inseam of pant-legs and airplane seats—will myself in sideways. As my chest and fingers scrape the wall, I can't help but think of that fucking Nutty Putty Cave diver who wound through the earth like a worm and trapped himself headfirst in a tunnel smaller than a washing machine, and I think *This is smaller than a washing machine* and feel my breath run thin remembering how the man's body was entombed in there, they just up and sealed the entrance, interred his stone-bruised corpse—Christ—they left him behind, in that algid, narrow place that snuffed him out like a flame inside the darkness.

While I am scraping my body along the narrow tunnel, dragging myself widthwise down several feet of space in agonizing motions, I strain to hear the wavering vinyl-in-reverse of unintelligible screaming from the opening on the other side. There is the sound of Pashmina saying something, hyperventilating murmurs, word-mulch pulped together, voice high and thin—*such is this* or *witch's kiss*—I can't tell what that woman is feverishly whimpering, but the fear in her voice makes my face hot with dread. I drag myself the last couple feet and squeeze inside the penumbra.

The room is ash-grey, lightless; illuminated only by the beam of our flashlight. It smells of thick, damp vomit here, and I see that she has puked, bile dripping from her lips. Pashmina's face has twisted into the ugly rictus of madness at the shock of seeing something unreal. She is still repeating the words, which I can finally hear, a moan of "What is this? What is this?" Again, and again, doubled over and face pressed into the palms of her hands. I take a moment to adjust to the dim and then nearly collapse.

A collective deathbed hallucination. It has to be. There is no way we are seeing what it is we are seeing. Neither of us wants to speak, least of all myself, already feeling the creeping fingers of insanity across my skull because, along with everything else I can *see*—I'm just close enough to it to be sure, in a confusing ever-shifting kaleidoscopic acid trip—the impossible. My granddad— who put a bullet through his head when I was eight—mummified in concrete, his not-face melted down, a loose and drooping eye socket into a mouth: the lopsided grin of another, and another; the hands of my mother and the eyes of my lover, a look, a gesture, a memory of a hundred other people I have known or dreamed or seen interwoven into a monolithic throne of faces and bodies in perdition, all half-soaked into the monochrome of the wall, where it no longer looks like concrete. It's flesh somehow, but not.

"Make it make sense," Pashmina is saying. "Make it make sense." Her voice is reaching fever-pitch as she sweeps the flashlight across the wall. Wherever our eyes fall, bodies are bubbling and stretching into metal and masonry, limbs and flakes of flesh like dough floating in hot oil, all of them in mid-gesture, like some sickening death dance, stone carapace victims among ruins or the Medusa-cursed.

And she flicks the moonbeam flashlight across the back of the room, and—

"Oh my fucking God—"

The room converges infinitely. Subtle patterns of skin interwoven into a single flesh, into stretched walls of nerves and limbs, faces, and then full bodies, seeping down and spilling onto the floor a mix of mortar and columns of membrane.

"No. No, no, no, no…" A quickening prayer like a metronome, as something moves—there is something *moving* in here, in this place that is utilitarian but seems more like a tomb. The huddled shape pools up, elongates into a figure, then turns.

Locks on us.

Sees us.

Sees us with white-hot eyes like burning stars in a night-bruised sky, a sharp cut of recognition.

It pulls, stretches its pelt so taut as to have holes in it. Then tears itself away from the wall, its wet edges flicking and popping like cooked fish skin.

Sounds leak out from deep inside it, inhuman, a long slew of words, low in pitch then rearing itself into a scream—a language unknown—a mournful voice, warning, pleading. Before it's too late.

The sound pierces me like a blade.

It scuttles across the threshold towards us. Stabs out the dark and slaps an arthritic grip around Pashmina's wrist. Its skin there, fat over day-old soup, clinging like a scab, and she recoils from its touch. Her hand darts out and punches at its torso, and it coughs out dried flesh into the air like spores.

Pashmina starts to scream.

Reams of madness pool out of an open seam inside me, one I'm not sure I can ever close up.

She had been leading the two of us until now, but she staggers back, drops the phone and threads herself back between the walls and out.

Fuck the phone. I ditch it and follow suit at the tail end. Years as an EMT have exposed me to plenty of mental shock, but nothing like this.

Pashmina is running, weaving through the labyrinthine station like a frantic rabbit. I'm so scared to take my eyes off of her, I'm not even keeping track of which way we're going. Not the way we came. Can't be, because the hall suddenly plunges down a narrow stairwell, an alarmingly claustrophobic aspect. Pashmina takes a sharp left at the second landing, so that I almost lose her. For a second I do.

And in that moment, flying down corridors, screaming a long-pitched wail distorted by nightmarish angles, Pashmina turns an entirely new corner—and meets the immediacy of an open chasm overspilling against eternal greys, before reversing out of reptilian fear.

She reels and hits my chest as I am blowing in around the bend just in time to see. And bowing forward, hard, folding over the waist-high balcony of cement, winded, knocked off her feet, she falls, falls, and there is a silence—a silence stretched too long as I grip the edges of the cavity in the wall she's just disappeared into—the world spinning like a carnival before her until she descends the dizzying height of a pit, and with a blow of exhalation hits the concrete floor with a meaty smack.

THE HORRIBLE SMELL OF Pashmina's piss and blood and excrement beams into my senses as I try to carry her on the unforgiving pilgrimage back to the station turnstiles, her miserable voice whispering in my ear, *Which way? But, which way?* And I don't know anymore. Through further junctures and forks in this maze of halls, I can't find my way back, ducking instead into a small room. If I think about that thing in there— those people, metabolized into the walls—for even a second, my skin flashes hot, then cold, and I feel my bowels clench up.

Pashmina has a compound fracture. Her leg is an open wound. Urine and feces dribble down into the opening between the skin and the muscle.

The bone shudders and shifts, as though something sickeningly cancerous is festering beneath the meat, but she doesn't seem to see.

"Fuck—my *leg*," she is moaning while I unravel the long spool of her scarf to wrap it with. She vomits again at just the sight of her jagged bone gouging out through the fabric of her pants, lacquered in blood, and this time it's nothing; it's thick, creamy bile because she's already thrown it all up before.

It's a direct line trajectory from this, through vitriolic arguments of who and what and where to go, but she says there is no way she is ever going anywhere near that room again, the room that's on a straight and narrow path to everything else, that she herself believed is most possibly an exit, and that leaves me in a bind.

Either way, with her leg broken, we are forced to hunker down for at least an evening until we can agree on a course of action. Her injury is at once relieving and terrifying. Relieving because pulling the EMT training to the forefront of my mind keeps me from thinking about more insidious things. Terrifying because I don't want to have to make the moral judgement of carrying her or leaving her behind if one of those things somehow finds us here. I try to make her comfortable with what little means I have. The only items we managed to pilfer from the *dép* are mineral water, some no-name-brand painkillers, a cheap bottle of vodka, and a handful of snacks, which she grabs from her bag—half-disintegrated protein bars crumbling around at the base of the fabric with lint and lozenge wrappers—and offers some to me.

Food is so unappetizing; I cannot. We sit on opposite ends of the room and try to sleep for a while. It drifts in starts and fits.

I AM UP BEFORE I know it, tearing the zipper down my hoodie as its flaps drop open like a ribbon. It is the middle of the night—it has to be—but some egg timer inside me has just dinged and I'm springing to action.

The torchlight of the overhead lights enflames the night, illuminating the stripped, deserted room. The scatter of blood and discarded food wrappers cuts across my vision and I stumble away, drawn to the nearest corner, regressing to something animal. It's a thirty-foot stretch across tiny hexagonal tile in dizzying grey. There is the raw, stabbing paranoia, odd and familiar, unfurling across my rib cage in constricting waves, like a rippling dilation of a pebble dropped into calm waters and the gentle squeeze of my intestines.

I drop to my knees and scramble desperately inside my pocket, find the familiar edges of a miniature tackle box where I keep my personal supply. My hand knows where to find the Xanax and I knock a couple back before I spiral because this is fucked. This is fucked. This is so fucked, and I know it, my body must know it, for fuck's sake, it's screaming at me to get out of here—it gave me the mercy of tender dreamless sleep but now it's had enough; the animal part has taken over, pumped me with adrenaline and panic like an unloaded gun. I feel like a horse in a slaughterhouse; all I want to do is run or scream or cry.

I'm trying to rationalize this shit. In me, an immense panic reigns. My thoughts race wildly, quicker than my heart. Am I dead? Did I drown at the Saint Lawrence River, just like I wanted, and this is some fucked purgatory Dante has dreamed up for me? Did Felix slip me some drugs? Am I infected with something? Is there a brain tumour pressed up against my skull giving me hallucinations? These seem improbable, impossible even, but then what is this? Where have I found myself?

A couple summers ago, I dropped acid at some chick I met at the laundromat's house party. She looked like a high priestess, so that's what I called her. I wanted so badly to feel something. To taste that ego death revelation New Age freaks always wax on about. You know: *eat acid, see God*—and, oh, I got that. Ten hours watching face-melting lovers kissing in the dark of some muggy womb-like room, their bare skin sizzling, waxy and puckered with spots like hives. The High Priestess, not enjoying her trip, but instead spending it babysitting me as I cried from the overwhelming discomfort. The trip snapped like kindling: from cool moth-like fractals to weird distortions, the world turning dream-to-nightmarescape, time stretching—nervous, tense, and achingly long. When lying down and closing my eyes was no reprieve, I started to dry-heave from panic, I dug into my pocket and took two Xanax. I read somewhere it was like a firetruck-red "*abort*" button that dropped a nuke on your high—which is absolute fucking *bullshit*, by the way, it does fuck-all—and I spent the rest of what felt like an eternity in comfortless terror.

That is the closest feeling I have to what I am experiencing here.

I press a hand to my chest and kiss my forehead to the ground, then snap back to a kneeling position of prayer when I think of the bodies half-absorbed in that room. I don't want to give this place any chance to take me.

My mind swims up and surfaces from the battlefield trenches of panic. There's the distorted wail again.

Like,

A whisper.

Tickling my brain.

It started and hasn't stopped since we arrived, can't possibly be something human; a persistent susurrant sound of some mighty engine with no breath, boring into my brain like a drill gun. The longer we stay, the louder it gets. I worry what will happen when the tide of it floods to its zenith.

When I am bored of grey tile and white noise, I straighten. I drop back on my palms and lower my ass to the tile. I am grateful for the floor's cool touch.

My gaze grazes across the unnatural greenish fluorescence of expansive space and lands on a figure. Pashmina. Pressed up against the corner of the room. Her eyebrows are up past the soft, misty silver curl of her fringe, and she looks oddly like a little shocked paper doll.

My face blanches. I stand. Move to greet her. I slump down beside her, dragging my legs up and clasping my palms loosely around my knees. The smell of piss and shit pollutes the room. I don't say anything about it. Her body is not a pretty sight, its deep suffering fulgurating to the surface of her like stars in a velvet-black sky, its pain provoked, made public and put on display.

She's surrounded by containers of vanilla pudding. Discarded, uneaten. I get that.

She stares past the threshold of the room at an escalator. It palpitates a gentle pulse like a beating heart each time the lower landing expels a serrated step. Overhead, inverted crenellations of concrete dissever further mezzanine landings and cut the harsh luminescence of the overhead lights into a lambent gloom. Looking over, it goes so far up. This single escalator where I carried Pashmina rises at least three stories, before turning off and disappearing around the left. We are small in this place; silence its judgement and indifference our condemnation.

"Vicodin?" she says, her voice thin and distant. It's the first thing she's said to me in hours.

"Xanax," I say. I slip the tackle box back into my pocket. "I'll be set for a while."

She fishes in her bag and pulls out a clear prescription bottle. The pills inside rattle as she raises it between her thumb and forefinger. "Percocet," she says.

My mouth forms a thin-lipped commiserative smile. "What's it for?"

It's relieving, in a sense, not to be the only one on medication here.

"The Big C," she replies. "I've got a tumour in my leg." She seems hesitant at first, her face drawn closed, but her eyes flit up to me, and she becomes an open book. What's the use in hiding anything here?

"I may not look like it, but I used to be lean muscle and rage. Then this… thing came out of fucking nowhere." She huddles the lapels of her jacket close like a Mylar blanket. "I hate getting old. It's just the progressive onset of random aches and pains that overstay their welcome like shitty in-laws. I was just sitting at my desk and then suddenly one day: chronic knee pain. What the actual hell, right? *Every single person* kept telling me I should go to a doctor. I'm not waiting sixteen hours in an ER just for some Extra Strength Tylenol. I don't think I was in denial; when you're younger, these things come and they go. I figured the pain would just disappear on its own. Then, one day I sat my ass on the toilet and—pop!—I broke my knee. Sitting on the toilet! Can you honestly fucking believe that?"

She waits for me to insist she carry on. When I don't, she waves a hand at me and scoffs bitterly.

"You can laugh. It hurt so bad I begged the doctor to kill me. Well, if you're still breathing and you've got a muff, they're so dismissive. All the doctors I've met or heard about do not take women's pain seriously. The attending nurse was also horrendous. And then they did an MRI and all of a sudden everyone was dancing to a very different tune."

"I mean—you hide it well." I wince at my poor choice of words. "What I mean to say is, I wouldn't have known."

"Ha! That would be the Percocet. I can barely believe the amount of medication I need every day just to function like everybody else." Her thousand-mile stare bores into the wall. "But things were finally fine for a while. Constipated as hell from the chemo and all that, and three years of surgeries, but it all becomes routine. You settle into this state of waiting. I busied myself with all those little things, the ones that rot you, wasting time running errands or sitting on my ass, watching *90 Day Fiancé*. None of the big dreams, no starting a goat farm or buying a private island or anything like that. And meanwhile time just…" She flutters her fingers. "Slipped away. Knowing about this *thing* changed nothing. You can't imagine how long it's been since I've let anyone touch me. By the time I realized I wanted a change of scenery it was too fucking late. It had extended into my nerves."

"That's not good," I offer limply.

"Uhh… no shit? They said it's very aggressive. Like an off-leash dog." She doesn't even look at me. Her eyes narrow and she fixes her gaze to a hexagon tile on the floor. "You know, I am very mentally resilient. I like to be in control."

I hadn't noticed.

She cuts her hand vertically through the air and hardens her gaze. "I decide when the ride starts, where and with who and how fast, and when I want to bail, and how—it's *my* fucking ride." The stiffness in her hand abates and it drops slack in her lap. "Imagine living like that and then suddenly you wake up to a phone call from a doctor saying he's gonna cut your leg off in the hopes that it'll take your chance of survival from three to eight percent. What could prepare one psychologically for that?"

She seems to be mourning her body's betrayal like a crushing bereavement. Trapped in a liminal state before her mind adjusts like a tuning fork to its new reality.

Her offerings of wildly vulnerable wells of personal information make me grimace with discomfort. I'm a little appalled at the thought of having a heart-to-heart exchange with a woman who found me thoroughly contemptible until just now, though, as an EMT, I know how trauma can greedily accelerate our capacity for intimacy.

"Will you do it?"

She gives me a sidelong glance. "You're a funny bunny. What choice do I have? You know, everything is normal, and then one day it's not." I'm not sure if she's talking about the station or her body until she continues: "That's how sickness can strike. It attacks with calculated indifference… it's exhausting. I really just…" She takes a deep breath and closes her eyes, tilting her head back. "… want to turn it off. I want to turn the whole fucking thing off."

I think of how this place is like a body: the melted corpses strewn, exploded cells, membranes splattered against the wall like crashing golden nebulae a million light years away. What would come of the two of us, if it were? A cluster of unknown cancerous cells bobbing around, aberrant malware, drifted past the event horizon of what could be considered healthy. Would the body rage against the foreign instruments? Isn't that what sickness is? A violence, in need of direction, channeled inward?

It doesn't seem so alien that way.

The very body that shelters you turns you away, a starving medieval pauper left begging on church steps. Even the language we use to describe sickness is, at its best, rife with rote metaphor, and, at its worst, profoundly dehumanizing. It inscribes a lack of control: we "battle" insomnia, we "suffer" a heart attack, become "victim" to dementia. We "collapse," at times even "succumb" to sickness. Yielding to death.

We aren't so different that way, Pashmina with her Percocet, me with my Xanax. A sickness in the mind is just as poisonous, can devour the body the same as a cancer. Trauma does not always carry big battle wounds. Sometimes it appears in the broad daylight of cold wars fought in silence. For this, I do not say anything to Pashmina, don't know if she wants to be comforted or left alone. I'd probably want to be left alone. She tells me she feels unmoored, by her illness, by this place. The whole winding of it. A maze to go mad in.

All of it has ushered us into a season of uncertainty. It nauseates her, she tells me, her own body turned viperous. Most of all, she laments the loss of beauty.

"Is that narcissistic?" she asks with a dry laugh, and I tell her no. We are all so eager to connect and to be loved. Our bodies feel like an external promise to that. Youth and health, both: they throb, expand, then disappear. The thought of it all pierces her heart so sharply it is like a lightning strike. She already grieves its disappearance—the filth that time finds in her pulse, gathering beneath her skin like a storm. Then, rising, it finds the shores of her like garbage on a tide. "Like, for real, fuck this," she says, and she chokes out a demented laugh like someone on the gallows. "I feel like my independence is gone—I don't even have a choice." Her eyes grow violent. "Makes me want to take it all back and nuke it to the ground as a huge fuck you. One big, fat *fuck you*."

L YING ON THE GROUND next to Pashmina. Insomnia pulses in me like jet lag, like an unspeakably large hunger that no feast could ever satiate.

I'm going to do some exploring. Might as well check out as much of it as I can in this lifetime. Life's short! Life's shorter when you're standing on the gallows.

Unequipped, peeking in, exploring at random. No matter where I walk, not a soul. Places like this really bring out the worst in people, so it's a bit of a relief.

An endless enfilade of rooms come, cells branching off halls. Straight and clean as open wrists. I'm almost certain if I took a sledgehammer to the wall that I would find more empty cells hidden within its compressive strength. This place really speaks to the value of a good exit sign.

Hey. What kind of room has no doors or windows? A *mush*room. *Ha-ha-ha*. Okay. Get a hold of yourself, moron. You get lost and you're as good as dust.

I try to put some distance between Pashmina and myself to explore the rooms she won't be able to walk to, and I find a couple of things. This place isn't as empty as it seems. I haven't found any rooms like the last, but there is a corridor with plain, grey doorless openings lining its halls, and the Coin Eye Skeleton hiding in there.

The Coin Eye Skeleton is a skeleton in the south hall. It doesn't scare me, which in all honesty I think is the Xanax shaking hands with my unfeeling depression. It's clothed in a fluffy pink overcoat, slumped off in the corner, sloughed clean of flesh and offal. Nothing in its pockets. The room itself is as drab and barren as the rest of this place. It has a noose tied round its neck, loose now from time, and two silver coins over its eyes. *Charon's obol*, I think. Coins for the ferryman.

I pluck one out of its orbital bone and pass my thumb over it. Tarnished Canadian quarter. Unremarkable. I feel bad for taking them, but I might need them later, so maybe they'll let me borrow them for a bit if they've already paid the ferryman. I pocket them.

My phone is gone and, having lost track of time, I have no sense of the hour. No one new shows up, so I try to make my way back to Pashmina. Lost, I can't exactly find the room, so I approximate. I make my way back to the original turnstile and try to find her from there. Pausing a moment, I peer across the landscape. Awe and overwhelm kiss each of my eyelids. Where do I even start?

I can't look at it for too long, but still I try to make sense of it. The architecture is of ludicrous proportions the way that brutalism always is: monolithic in its oppression. Heavy. A series of underground interiors with atriums so tall as to give simultaneous cases of claustrophobia and agoraphobia. From where I stand with my back to the kiosk, it looks like a perspective painting, walls and ceilings cut and grooved into slanting rays of cement, stairs incised at odd angles fanning out like blades.

Architectural schematics tilting onto their side—looking up a spire, or down a well, or lengthwise at a set of spinning stairs, which aren't even stairs at all, but just a decorative detail along the wall. The whole thing hurts to look at. I am sure if I move closer to it that it might break the illusion. Or worse yet, I might see some great big eye pull out from between two walls, see the silhouette of some unfathomable eldritch thing watching me, and the thought of this, alone, forces me to turn away.

I don't need this. What I need is the calm cool release of more Xanax, because I've been shoved in here like an afterthought, teetering on the edge of hysteria.

I duck into one of the many small, dim rooms, and swallow down some more Xanax, then slump languid in one of the corners the colour of November rain pebbled with grey. I sit gazing down the pipeline of interconnected corridors, punched through with windows—the safety and comfort of smooth, blank walls, the converging landscape of indifference, of normal, waiting for the dumb, dizzy blur of calm to wash over me. That's all this ever is: waiting.

I skate along the surface of sleep, dreams of lamprey distilled by the warped distortions of sound. A tiny hole punctures through the veil of slumber. It's a strain to keep my eyes open, tired from the trip, and laden with stress, but when I do I can see, through the haze of the windowless door separating the rooms, a ripple on the lake of grey-on-grey interior of the second or third room, slinking along. Far away, so far away and hard to care when the sleep of Xanax is so good. I close my eyes and open them and it's still there. Manifesting plump pale flesh wrapped in ice-pink crushed velvet. It's pretty. So pretty, like an angel. I could cry. Light and nimble, fluid, soft. It's a girl, I realize. The High Priestess New Ager from some summers ago.

Our eyes meet and she smiles. She presses her finger up against her lips, our little secret, then tips back into the shade, where the room swallows the light, and she disappears.

ND WHEN I WAKE, everything is heightened.

I'm struggling to make sense of what's happening, until reality decompresses in my brain like a crash collision airbag. There's this distorted gurgle through ruptured lungs that warbles in and out of the sound overhead, roaring over my Xanax tinnitus.

It's coming from Pashmina. She's wailing—I realize with a seizing breath—I haven't lost her at all. No, in fact, in my stupor I must've somehow looped around, and she's been in the cell beside mine the entire time I've been sleeping.

I tear myself out of my room, and dive into hers, then reel wildly from the sight.

Immediately regret.

I am too close. The room is suffocatingly small for my broad build; I don't know how I ever slept here with her before, because now it's tiny, choking me with its reek—some briny mix of rust and stomach acid, the alchemy of which makes me want to gag— and I crash my head against damp wool. My feet mire in a twist of fabric, catching on something slippery, and I fall into a puddle of it, like socks on cold cat vomit. I can feel its wetness overlap and seep under the cuff of my pant-leg, in and around my wrists and ankles, and bleat out a sound like a panicked animal.

I look around into the caliginous room, full and dark as a womb and—oh, fuck—more vast than sea or stars, Pashmina has expanded somehow, skin thinned like rolled parchment, her veins visible, moulting the skin of her back into wings, stuck to the wall, tearing and pulling away at the back of her ankles, and there is no reason for it, no reason at all why it would have happened to her above me.

The room's canted angles dim the shape of her in a fevered nest of her scarf, like it's multiplying, but still the silhouette looks wrong. It's like the space is sucking the colour out of her scarf, out of *her*, and it seems to mesh its fabric patterns in nauseating swirls into her skin.

She has thrown the cover off her makeshift sleeping bag and is balancing her weight on her elbows. The meat and skin of her legs have sloughed off the bone like a detonated grenade and pooled into a marbling thick pink-grey liquid of flesh and poured concrete. Pashmina hears my panicked, choking gasps and sweeps on the tide of it towards me.

She makes a convulsive reach for me, snatches at life with hideous voraciousness, and her upper torso shudders with strain, then rips away just below her navel. Her spinal column snaps, wishbone-crack, and a ream of blue-white entrails unspool from the open orifice before, finally, it all starts to melt.

Her mind is no more. She is enmeshed into the infinite grey landscape of this place, her body sunken into cement floor, and what remains is merely a husk. A stalagmite of a shape—reaching; sighing; wanting; as if it's expressing a wish to be anything at all, but that's all it is.

A ND THEN I AM alone.

The days stretch long.

God, help me, please. Everywhere I look around me, I feel sick. After the incident with Pashmina, I run out of Xanax almost immediately. She is a stone statue, reduced to a twisted menacing figure blazing at the ceremonial centre of the great room, and I snap, taking as much medication as I have. Which isn't to say much, there aren't many pills left, and when I'm completely out, it's like a light in me has finally been snuffed and I see this place for the magnitude and scope that it really is.

I try to climb back to the room with the far-reaching, narrow hall of cloying stench and half-humans rippling that mosquito-high crescendo of pitch like a thousand converged throats, but I'm unable to find the seam in the wall. If it's the only way out of here, I have to find it and push my way through before I change my mind. I search. For days, it feels. The skeleton is gone, or I'm getting my rooms confused, and I'm worried I've lost my mind, that I've imagined it somehow, but the coins are still there—in my pocket. With Felix's ticket. It's hard to count the time when the fluorescence causes an unsleeping artificial sun, and when I do find that hall where Pashmina and I once stood, there is no longer a foot-wide seam. It's closed itself, somehow, like blood cells have come in and clotted the station's wound tissue. Now it's just a hairline crack along the eastern wall, weeping a clear fluid down its surface, which hints of that lingering smell. I kick and I claw and I plead but the fissure does not split, and it is then that I realize I am really alone.

There's no getting out of here. There's no way out.

I feel like it's somehow all my fault.

Between shitting and eating and wandering about, there is nothing—no *point*—in being here, and without *purpose* there is no *happiness*; this is what my therapist always says. So in order to give myself purpose, I've started mapping the interior of this place. I force myself to look at spaces that have little visual appeal: the boring but sinister mechanical walkways with their catch basins at the base; the greige tile whose optic pattern intensifies towards the mezzanine; the ride of fluorescence ascending the easternmost staircase. It's like endlessly looping through an M. C. Escher casino.

When I'm able to recall from memory the layout of the initial dozen rooms, I move on to the next one, and the next. Continuing on—walking to do something nice for myself, but in Pashmina's absence cements my relapse. The prodrome of my punctures and perforations. The ugly splinter of it burrowing deep within me, such dangerous desperation for me to carve it out and *feel human*: all these mornings without sun, bored and filled with a furious rage, but numb—so numb—plagued by emotional anorgasmia.

Looking down now, weird sensation, like there's a heaviness sleeping beneath my skin. I feel as though I've swallowed rocks, over the top of it filaments of petal-thin membrane seamed together with paper-thin rind. Scaly erythema patches over my forearms and thighs have erupted into grey knots of flesh, beads of indurated papules threatening to pustulate at the centre. Around them, my skin is cold and pale, a thin layer of dermis painted over stone. Any paler and I'd be dead. It is intolerable, so intolerable I'm almost certain it's rotting me away from the inside.

I try to resist, but it trails at my back like a phantom. When I begin to cut, raking out wounds with a chip of cement, I'm not sure if it is to exorcize it from my body, or wake it from its slumber. I commit myself to colour. I'm trying to paint this grey place red.

The body can speak without words or tears. It does, like this. Paints patterns in an alchemy of illness across my skin. Sometimes I add to it, collaborative, unseaming gorges between the dotted points along my limbs. Wine-dark blood blooms from the channels. It's beautiful and sad, the brain versus body fight. The body holds divinity, but the brain seals the gates of its heaven.

It sickens me. These things that we do to ourselves.

M Y RELATIONSHIP TO FOOD here is fucked. It was bad before but now it's worse: eating the same thing repeatedly until I'm tired of it. And man, am I fucking tired of yogurt oats. *Dép's* only got junk food, which is fine for me—like I said, I haven't got the energy to cook—but when I do eat, and it's rare that I do—everything tastes like ash. Even water has a weird taste. Like metal.

Food is never so unappetizing as it is in this place. The result of which makes me feel hideous. I shed my weight like a deciduous forest when the nausea finds a season in me, my arms and legs whittling down to lanky canted angles, bony shoulders and visible sternum. I try to eat whatever I can stomach, walking through maintenance stairwells, doors and halls, each perfectly identical, until I find the next *dép*. There I can mush food into slurries so I can choke them back quick before I realize what I'm doing because here all food has the same sickening consistency as wet cat vomit, and it feels like a harvest of mottled, rotted fruit festers in my stomach.

I sit and stare at the grey flecks in the floor tile before my brain times out and one more sip makes me sick. This place takes everything from me. Life's simplest pleasures—eating, sleeping, sex—turned feculent.

A ND THEN: A SURREAL, magical moment. I'm trapped, exploring a long tunnel, the force of whose labyrinthine length is broken by varying widths and heights. When it finally ceases, it is into a large space with church-like grandeur, practically a work of abstract sculptural art, and astonishing angular proportions. The walls rise up in sombre grey concrete, as if in a twisted dream. They are patterned with vertical ridges. The only entryways: the concourse behind me and, across the chasm of wide-open space, another cavity to continue the tunnel on the other end.

Present at the top of a pointed dome in the centre of the ceiling like a keyhole into heaven, there it is: a skylight. It lets through a shaft of daylight, as a camera obscura, shining like a flame. It's the first time I've seen the open sky in this place, and though the light is the colour of cinderblocks, bleached of its brilliant blue hue by clouds, I am swaying, standing there, elated by the hint of open air. Though I soon find this is truly a deeply cruel discovery: a prohibited exit, so high up it's out of reach.

I yell up at it, furious, weary, cheated of reprieve: great acoustic experience, but not a soul in sight. It is essentially a jail cell window. I, the inmate. I pace and fume beneath it. There's a weak hope that if there is natural daylight I am close to some other exit I can climb out of. Is it worse to be a prisoner in a cell with a window or without?

The light hangs heavy above me. I stand beneath it and close my eyes. It's too far to warm my face but I try to sit with the feeling, even if it is make-believe.

Mandalas of red beneath shifting eyelids, ribbons of brilliant and saturated shades of vermillion confirm that I'm alive. That I am.

But also, the dual agony of it is that I feel every ounce of it. Every toothache, the weight of my head on my neck and gravity's ceaseless strength, the dryness between my hands, my joints. The pressure of it is building, hardening. Like a chrysalis my body is forming from my nervous system. I start with my extremities, slicing fresh gashes in the palms of my hands. Beautiful blooming red! And then it hits this atmosphere and oxidizes, wilts to the colour of thunder. I can't get it out.

Being in this, it's like seeing a colour no one else can. Some forbidden shade, heard only in whispers, friends of friends that have seen it, as though speaking the name of that particular pigment of vermillion might hex the world into an achromatic of only that—but not seeing that shade reflected anywhere. Well, it's maddening. It's worse than it not existing, because it very much does; some days I even feel like I'm drenched in it.

So I was surprised when it was grey, so much grey. I always thought it would be red. But I suppose blood when numbed and reduced like vinegar to a grisaille base is, just as anything else, grey as gunmetal.

I find myself in that room for hours. Time does pass; the sky deepens to a velvety black. When I can't see anymore, I move on. It's all just grey anyway. What use is a window if you're standing in the dark?

PAIN IS A GOD the body worships. I have been thinking about this phrase for a couple days now.

I believe it because I have knelt at its altar.

Before here, I would spend all day at work and have no energy when I got home to do anything, not eating and certainly not cooking, so I'd order in, and pick and prod at takeout until I'd toss it. Then I'd feel like shit—compound shit, if you will, from the original depression plus the guilt of buying food just to trash it—so I'd spend the rest of my money on a shrink to explore manifestations of my nervous mind, executive function disorder screwing with my ability to digest food, "*perfectly common, you know*," which meant I'd have no more money, so—! I'd go back to work and spend all day there trying to make enough to afford the shrink. Round and round I went. I'd get even more depressed about it, and that would fuck with my system—that's what a body is—a *system* your brain turns against itself—turns against *you*. Further, that's what torture is: autonomy removed, displaced—and pain, yes, but mostly the body turned mutinous. Most torture is actually pretty simple. It doesn't require any instruments or gadgets, only a little creativity.

Here, do me a favour. To sharpen your understanding, try this: well all the spit inside your mouth—now swallow.

Now do it again.

Now, again—don't waste time, just swallow whatever saliva is in there. Four, five times is kind of annoying, but regulate that to a hundred—a thousand? For days on end—weeks, months? Now can you see exactly what I mean when I say the body doesn't need much to simultaneously turn itself into your oppressor—into the site of your oppression?

I certainly can, for my body is a stranger to me sometimes. Butcher and bystander. That is what it is to be mentally ill. In this place, I stop eating, stop sleeping, feel exhausted, feel my blood is on fire, feel dizzy, nauseous, develop a fever, develop tremors and a rushing heart. The first time this happened, I was seventeen. I cycled through a revolving door of doctors and WebMD articles trying to identify my condition. Now I know what it is, but there's an added symptom: the knotted harbour of stone that scorches within my bones. It's seeping into my veins.

I keep it to myself. Isolated. If I ever said anything about it with any modicum of specificity in the before times, people would change the subject. Simultaneously, when people hear of pain, they think they're experts—what is one pain but another transposed?—and so, they welcome themselves in with the bravado of seasoned veterans and the solemnity of holy bishops, delighted to share the latest salves and surgeries. Medical specialists flinging procedures and prescriptions at you—betahistines and SSRIs, SNRIs, benzos and CNS depressants, DNRIs, rTMS, ECT, CBT, DBT—if the list seems inexhaustive, it's because it is, all sorts of fancy-colour pills that nuke your libido and make your limbs tense up with a writhing athetosis. Besieged by waves of nausea, I have never wanted to kill myself more than when I was on sertraline. Okay, that's not true, or I wouldn't be here, but regardless, it's a war you just can't win. Of course, the thoughts are worse here. How can they not be? Its endless maze of concrete, its skylight caisson taunting me. God damn this place! Here, in this fleshless belly of a whale, I am rinsed of the colour of the world. Here, I am more exhausted and listless than ever, marching the treadmill of lint-grey halls. Here, I have nothing to look forward to. And I am so monumentally lonely. I keep telling myself I'm waiting to get out and find the Saint Lawrence River to put an end to this life, but it almost feels like an excuse at this point. I could just as easily take a tumble off a concrete perch and fall to my death. So... why don't I?

Couldn't tell you. What I can tell you is: waking and sleeping have ceased to be distinct states. With or without medication, the insomnia of this place is monstrous. I'm plagued with a fatigue so immense, so inhuman, I don't know how my body contains it. When I rub my chest, I can feel something cold and firm flowering up from my ribs.

Blood coalesces and fractals in welts along my breastplate. There is something underneath it, cuspid bumps crawling beneath my skin. It's just a stasis, I tell myself—a pupal phase, rising from within.

I can feel it reaching, an inky blotch of what plagued Pashmina's body, unfurling down her spine like rosary beads.

It's going to take me pretty soon. I keep walking like I'm going to get somewhere but I never do. These rooms: creatureless. So deep in a maze of concrete walls, I might as well be a soul in perdition. I've even lost sight of Pashmina, the skeleton, the subway platform at this point. All tethers to reality: completely cut. I feel like I'm so far gone, I don't even know what the hell I'm doing to myself anymore.

I am suddenly struck with the sharp and terrified desperation to tear it out. When the morbid curiosity takes possession of me, I score lines into my existing wounds, lashing marrow-deep. It grants itself purpose in the serrated edge of the cement chip, the rickshaw scuttle against my skin, brandishing the lightest pain, violet-hot like a papercut. Am I still human? Will I bleed red or grey? I want the cuts and gashes to reveal what's inside: a numbing blaze of concrete, possessing such a weight that when I do walk into that body of water, big and blue, I'll sink straight to the bottom.

THE PERPLEXING LACK OF landmarks continues to plague me. I follow the western wall, traveling up escalators and down others, down the depth of a dungeon, to immense concourses, these strange sunken cathedrals with soaring ceilings held up by monumental concrete pillars staring coldly back at me. I'm entirely alone, but I'm worried if I cease movement, I'll run out of steam and the slate-grey mouth of this place will close up and devour me whole. I fear I will one day wake up embraced in a crushed stone cast, and be trapped against the floor, like a lone lover in the wreckage of Pompeii.

It is so much dull grey that all I can focus on is the paresis of my body, the nucleus of it decanting a grievous anesthetic venom through my nervous system, down my limbs and into my chest and hands, where I'd begun to carve.

The agony of it is sickening. I had placed a gauze pad from one of the *déps* against my chest a while back, kept in place with bandages wrapped around my torso, and it makes my swollen core feel much too big. Every time I touch it, I want to recoil; it's got an ungainly shape and I feel like a horrific mutant.

I undo the heart dressing. Beneath it is a checkerboard of cuts bathed in a gore so sickly I instinctively flinch away. I can't feel it, almost like it isn't mine, isn't my body at all. I palpate my sternum and the flesh bounces back tenderly. The closer I get to the wound, the one I cut into the other day, the less I can feel, until I can't feel anything, nothing, not a single thing, and I'm almost certain it's radiating outward—that it's grown since the last rest stop. I'm watching myself fade by degrees, the cement growing in its conquest, gradually turning my neck and shoulders numb.

Sometimes I wonder what can possibly come next. Who would have ever imagined Dante's *The Wood of the Self-Murderers* be husks entombed in poured concrete? And who would've imagined those trees bloom, not of planted seed, but of petrified souls, dispossessed of the bodies that allowed them to take in life's technicolour splendour? Stained-glass cathedrals smashed and reduced to inexorable decay.

Across the topography of my skin are lacerations for each room I transgress without exit. I cut and slash to make sure I'm still apart. To make sure I'm moving. A dozen already, tapered incisions crawling along my thigh. And then I hurl myself against the wall. The bruises that appear are just as grey. I'm gathering dust like a derelict factory. I hook my nails into the lip of an old cut on my thigh and stretch the hairline crack open to peer at what's inside. It fights against my hands, the flesh there a leaden, bloodless stump. Unseamed, I'm certain all that might float out are heaps of fine grey particles, like cremated remains in the urn of my body. Tough, pink meat glistens underneath, so okay, maybe it is fine—is healing, even—but I can feel it climbing up into my brain. The folds of it are already grey—juicy, but grey. I think it might've even started there.

EVERYTHING THAT MAKES ME feel good simultaneously makes me feel lost.

Do you ever think about how often you might appear in someone else's fantasies? Has anyone ever dreamed of you in the ways in which you dream of others? Obsessively trained on the thought of adding yourself to a photograph, a memory, a moment. Someone else yearning so much for the touch of your skin, wanting you so strongly you can feel the sense of it ghost over you as you sleep.

Maybe, with Felix from the subway. But it's stupid to assume we could ever be what others want. Crushes are dangerous in that sense. We think of other people in ways that put them on a pedestal. Is it weird to think of a stranger like that? In hunger? I don't think there's anyone who remembers me.

I've heard it said that a labyrinth is most pleasing to the ones viewing it from above. What do you say, old friend? Do you remember if he even looked back when the doors shut? Is there a juicy centre to this Tootsie Pop or am I deluding myself? This make any lick of sense from your cosmic perspective?

Sometimes, I think there are moments in life that are so memorable to me because of their impact, only to later find that they were forgotten by others almost immediately. What scars some is but a glance off the armour to others. The brightly burning Polaris of your life is nothing but a dim star, already faded and forgotten, in the descending dawn of someone else's.

In that sense, I suppose what sustains me is schmuck-bait. It may as well be. Felix, whose subway ticket is in my pocket, leads to what, exactly? A date with someone who's going to recoil in revulsion the moment I stop curating my marketable traits, when he sees the state I live in, that I speak to no one, that I give the world nothing. Knocked down a peg and then another. Not falling off the pedestal as much as tripping off like an imbecile in a silent film. I maintain that there's nothing worse than letting someone get to know you.

And often, these small defiances of expectations are not enough anyway. Oh, yes, yes, I know—the tools. The tools to fight! With a bit of radical acceptance/self-compassion/behavioural therapy/ mindfulness meditation and the right combination of diet and pills, you, too, can find the fucking exit to this place! Are you buying any of this shit?

Of course I want to be better.

The sheer fucking mental resilience it takes me to keep walking is nothing short of Olympic. It steals hours away in piecemeal increments. How can I run when what terrorizes me is everywhere? It doesn't come and get me; it just presents itself. It waits in plain daylight for the day I am too exhausted to say no.

I feel like I've completely lost my compass. I don't know what to trust anymore.

You? Sure.

Grant me that palliative cocktail of words. Go on, then. We'll violate performance convention and, for good measure, I'll even try to believe you. Tell me that taking note of these things is progress and that progress isn't linear.

Tell me there are people who can endure the magnitude of this space. Tell me I can be one of them. Tell me there are brutalists who will love the renaissance of concrete in me, who'll find solace in the smooth abstraction of cement. Tell me there are those who wish to decorate the walls of this station with scarlet-red dahlias. Tell me some of those dahlias will bend towards the shade. Tell me I can map this place out. Tell me that with enough strength I can peel the walls like an orange. Tell me I'm not beyond help. Tell me the horseshit I tell myself to get through the nights isn't the impulse of a hopeful delusion. Tell me we're supposed to care. And then—and this is the key part—tell me that everyone's just doing the best they can. Insist on it. Because the truth is, aren't we?

You see, now, why I didn't want to get distracted? A hairline crack of optimism. All that it took to sink the *Titanic* was a two-foot slice in the wrong compartment. Two feet, in the body of a steel titan. Rendered unmade in just under three hours.

Listen, let's be real, I am not so fucking delusional as to think one man can solve all my problems. We've all been in romantic relationships before and still felt lonely. Just look at my parents. Co-dependency is nothing but a survival tactic and thus far I have been so very, very good at surviving. So much so, I am starting to feel the curse of consciousness, of remorse. The stupid, dim flicker of hope.

Absurdly, now, I think of that time I visited Lake Kawaguchiko with my mom, our evening walks a tradition, when filming among a sleepy grassland we had seen the blue-white sequins of three shimmering stars, impossibly perfect: a tapestry of pinprick silver jewels stitched into the sky, lucent as the eyes of distant suns. We were so sure we were seeing something alien, like Phoenix Lights, the furious milky glow of some far-off spaceship.

I caught it on camera, of course. Always with the home movies—that was my *thing*; I held everything tightly, captured it with film, freezing the ephemeral forever, those videos a type of preserved secret. I grasped it all with such fervour. Catching it in that moment on that cheap Hi8, the awe of my mom off-screen cleaving "*Sweet-pea, look! Look! Are you getting it?*" into the sky. And then, we'd gone back home where I'd looked it up and saw it was the mapping of a constellation—the Summer Triangle— three of the brightest stars, between them a bridge to unite lost lovers. It was all so beautiful.

And, you know, years have passed since then.

I still miss my mom.

I still miss the stars.

I don't want to die in a place with no stars. Grief bubbles in me like a trapped body of air. The stupid thoughts spill out convulsively. It doesn't matter. For any of it to ever work, I'd have to get rid of this. And I've been dead for so long, I don't know if I can come alive again.

ACOUPLE YEARS BACK A woman named Elisa Lam went missing while on a trip to Los Angeles. Kind-eyed, lively and friendly, she had been staying as a guest at the Cecil Hotel in downtown LA. Hotel staff say she was alone. The air that day was warm. Sunny. Her last sighting was by a clerk at The Last Bookstore, buying souvenirs for her family.

A week after she vanished, flyers were posted online and in the neighbourhood to bring it to public attention. The police searched the hotel and its surroundings, and came away empty-handed. Two weeks later, in the hopes of finding her, the LAPD released surveillance footage from the hotel elevator. The footage is an unsettling watch. Two-and-a-half minutes of Lam, alone, behaving strangely: pressing what appears to be all the call buttons, peeking around the open doors, hiding herself as small as possible in the corner of the elevator. During the police search, hotel guests began complaining of weak water pressure. Then, of water discolouration and strange taste. Later, a hotel maintenance worker found something in one of the hotel's rooftop cisterns providing water to guest rooms, a kitchen, and a coffee shop. Through the open hatch, they saw the marbled, bloated corpse of an unidentified woman floating face-up in the water. It was Lam.

To this day, no one knows exactly how she died.

What we do know is that the bizarre and disturbing nature of the whole thing blazed like a wild grease-fire across the web, funneled viral by a fuel jettison of "likes" and "shares" like cooking oil. The internet age has helped new crops of dark and dangerous urban legend games spread like wildfire, and they've dialed up the danger elements considerably.

One of the theories of her death included the Elevator Game: a ritual game, which, allegedly, allows players to slip through the veil into a haunted realm that is not our own. Like most sinister games, it's got very simple rules, at least if you live in a city.

Here's how you play.

MATERIALS:
You
A ten-story building with an elevator

INSTRUCTIONS:
To start the game, players must enter the elevator at the first floor.

Press the button for the second floor. Do not proceed if anyone enters or exits the elevator. If they do, start over from the beginning.

Press the fourth floor.

Press the second floor.

Go to the sixth floor.

Press the tenth floor.

Press the fifth floor.

If a woman enters at the fifth floor,

DO NOT LOOK AT HER.

DO NOT SPEAK TO HER.

The person is not a person.

Do not exit the elevator. Press the button for the first floor.

If the elevator descends, then the ritual has failed. Exit the elevator and don't look back. Try again another time.

If the elevator ascends, then the ritual has succeeded. When you reach the tenth floor, you will find yourself in another world. Although this place may seem similar, you will notice that the only one present is you. If the woman from the fifth floor asks where you are going, do not answer her. Whatever you do, do not look at her. You are welcome to explore the ascension realm, but do not lose sight of the elevator.

And… that's it. After which, it's just you and your shadow. It's kind of a voluntarily eating Tide Pods situation, but aren't all urban legends kind of like that? And anyway, as expected, people play at their own risk.

I've been too chickenshit to play in full. A grown man, too scared to try a children's game. Chalk it up to childhood trauma, that wild illusive fear that still festers under our skin from moments in darkened closets and basement cellars; the terrifying flash of a lightbulb snap; the glimpse of a heavy shadow snatching at us from the oily dark. The one rule of urban legends always seems to be they must be experienced in isolation—it always seems to work better that way. I guess ghosts are best reckoned with in solitude, and we work best to meet them there; only in that twilight of drowned silence can we hear them linger.

I feel a bit of a connection to Lam's solitude, so I say: let's resurrect that old feeling.

All of which is to announce:

I've found an elevator in here.

At first, it really feels like I've lost it. It's been a while since I've seen a break in the monotony of cement; there's been no *dép* for some time, not even any maintenance stairwells or stalagmite people, and so the appearance of an elevator is disorienting. My hands tremble at the sight of its smooth, silver face in the wall. The prospect of something new thrills me. When you're in a place like this, you'll jump at any slight opportunity for something to shake things up a bit, feel like you're not being frescoed into the landscape itself.

It's a commercial elevator, small, with plain call buttons, lacking any distinct markings except direction indicators. Unceremoniously, I hover my finger over the call button. My body chills, the squeeze of excitement edged with terror, childlike fright—

and I press.

I'd be surprised if this shit is even functional, but as my finger hits, there is a second of silence and then the motor rumbles to life, churning the cables, deploying the elevator.

The very air feels serrated with long, sharp needles.

The elevator dings, and the doors glide open.

It's narrow.

And empty.

I don't know if that's disappointing or not. I step inside, working slowly, like when you've got too much time to kill between obligations at a mall, and you linger a little around everywhere, just long enough to seem over-invested in the very mundane.

The walls are all reflective chrome, smudged with fingerprints and dried, milky stains. There's a couple rows of convex disks for floors, some partially worn down, and door controls topped with Braille plates. There is an alarm button (which I *don't* press—I feel like I'm savouring that for later, boredom-edging, maybe), and from the looks of it, I am on Ground, which has a little silver star next to it. When I consider how deep underground I must be, I scoff.

The only other weird thing one might misconstrue as dangerous is that there's a lingering smell in here. Arid. A cloying almond-bitter trace, almost gastric—same as in that hall with the bodies—but that's all. Nothing else.

I stand there for a second and the doors glide shut. It sits, waiting for input.

Now, will you play, they say. No shit! Of course I'm going to play. What's the worst that can happen? I die? Great punchline, jackass.

The whole thing has me a little manic, I'll be honest; the way you get giddy when you're sleep-deprived—which I am—and develop an addled god-complex that rivals that first hit of blow. I'm suddenly really into this idea of playing the Elevator Game, feeling a little mythic; a little David meets Goliath, or probably Theseus and his Minotaur.

Life suddenly takes on a gilded tint, the glowing potential of danger and excitement and adventure—*would you like to meet a ghost?*—I'm chuckling, talking to myself; I've always loved that line, that early-internet glory. You could be clicking shit on Rotten dot com without having a goddamn clue about what it is that you were diving into, something titled motorcycle.jpg, expecting the obvious, which wasn't anything of the sort, but was (now, quite famously) a picture of a failed suicide attempt, shotgun to the face—and, *survived!* Talk about maniac—that's not the way I'd like to go, calm and cool for me: right into the ocean, remember? And this adrenaline rush has me feeling like a junkie; I just hope I can remember the order of this game right, but it's easy enough, even numbers first then mid, top, bottom, me and her—the silver lady—gliding up and down, I'm yo-yoing between floors, and figures, no one comes in, so fuck it—! Up and down and up and down and I'm laughing my ass off, 'cause obviously there's nobody there. The door never shuts unless I tell it to; it's just me and you, silver baby! And I'm pressing four, then six, then five; this is where the needle drops, and you think it's going to but it *doesn't*, hahaha, it doesn't! That's fucking life for you! You sign yourself up for some fun, exciting shit, something quite possibly dangerous, and it doesn't even deliver! Holy shit, I'm cracking up at this, whole thing manifest—a whole entire-ass subway station and it couldn't even give me a morsel of excitement; like, you'd *think* doors would open on ten to one of those creatures hobbling at me, Pashmina, even, a face not so unfamiliar—it's capable of so much! It's like a datamoshed wet dream but it can't even make this one thing! It's like it's doing it on purpose. And man, I am fucking *howling*. No wristwatch, losing track of time, just up and down and up and down, like that fucking kid in China who kept tampering with the elevator doors, forcing them open with the foot of his umbrella, again, again, again, until the shit just said *ça suffit*, 'cause even machines have their limit, and it just closed the doors and bit down on his umbrella handle like a fucking bulldog and supposedly dove into a free-fall.

Would you like to meet a ghost? Wouldn't that be swell?

Up and down and up and down, dizzyingly, me whooping and laughing. Every floor, the same bewildering absence of landmarks, grey and colourless, the same interminable blow-your-brains-out bullshit. And now, yeah, maybe I did look like Elisa Lam, peeking in and out of the elevator and hiding off in the corner. Hiding from what? The smooth blank walls of exactly nothing. Floors seem to flash by in a montage, each scarcely different than the last, open, close, up, down, up again; it gets to a point where I'm frantic and delirious, and I'm about halfway through when my hand freezes in the air, finger poised above the eighth-floor call button.

Listening, I can't tell if I can hear someone vocalizing or if I'm actually losing it. There's stories of that, you know? People hearing songs of angels in tinnitus.

Either way, the novelty of it paralyzes me. The doors are closed and I'm traveling down so the sound has only one orientation with which to roll. It expands, finds direction. Cataloguing its location: down a couple floors, but moving pretty swiftly. It is clearly a voice now. A jolly tune I recognize but can't place the name of. A sort of jovial Boy Scout song, something nostalgic of war era mounted on the parade-march pulse of footfalls. And I can hear the words, faintly, as the elevator purrs down towards the voice on the floor below, then louder: "*Valderi, valdera! Valderi, valdera-ha-ha-ha-ha-ha!*"

Like the speeding ticks of a Geiger counter. A Pied Piper tune, which fills me with fear the closer it gets. I feel the hot flash of dread—like a premonition—that this is something dark careening my way, and I can't help but hurtle, helplessly, full-force into it. I thought exhaustion and boredom had dulled my delicate capacity for fear, but not so! It's creeping in under my skin like a fever, and I'm ramming my finger against the buttons between this floor and that, but the elevator's had enough of my nonsense and is barreling down to it.

Part of me is thinking, *At least I'm not alone.* Part of me is thinking, *At least there are others.* They had to have come from somewhere. A way out. A way out, and if not, at least real-life company in this refracted rat maze. Only that's not comforting, not in the way it should be.

But then, my head's all messed up from dancing between floors, my choices mercurial, and all that fills my head is:

Would you like to meet a ghost?

Stupid fucking movie quotes. Brain rot is what it is, no room up in my noggin for CBT's *Healthy Perspectives on Emotion*; it's all filled with soundbites of crap I saw on the internet.

The voice sounds very close—on this floor, now—and just as I think this, the elevator ceases with a thunderous bang, and abruptly, so does the singing. As though the song's been sucked out of the air. There is complete silence. My eyes dart over to the control panel, and I see we're on five.

Oh, fuck, I think wildly. The doors open and I put my head down and stare between my feet.

All I can think of are the rules of the game:

DO NOT LOOK AT HER.

DO NOT SPEAK TO HER.

THE PERSON IS NOT A PERSON.

Everything is deathly still. Lakewater, as a beast churns beneath.

And then there are the footfalls of someone crossing the threshold into the elevator and the doors closing. They stand to my left, and all I can see, as their arm bisects to hit the tenth floor, is they're holding a cherry-red plastic cup of something. I'm trying not to look—does this count?—does this count as looking?—and all I can see is a time-weathered hand holding this cup of what at first I think must be beer, but no, it isn't—it can't be—what's there is churning in its basin: thick, gooey treacle sloshing along the edges of the plastic cup. Its scent punches up into my nostrils with a nauseating reek. My face scrunches and I squeeze my eyes shut.

Caustic soda. It's caustic soda.

"Where are you going?" the singer says. Their voice splits between octaves, like double-exposed film. Distant. Textured.

Do not speak to her. The person is not a person.

If I don't go there myself, it's trying to lead me there. My body. I don't say anything. I told you what I wanted was the waves. Don't usurp my decision with another.

I feel light-headed. I almost drank caustic soda once, and this smell is strobing dark and unwanted memories across the insides of my eyelids like a crime scene. My eyes flutter beneath their lids and I catch a vivid glimpse. This person's got pills in one hand and the drink in the other. They're facing the wrong way. Their back is to the door. I don't see anything else. I don't want to.

The elevator chimes.

"Won't you join us on ten?" they ask.

The doors open and I think I can hear music, like an office party or something. I can't tell if the voices are from a song, or guests, or my own hysterical psychosis. I don't open my eyes, so I don't see it. I keep them clenched shut. I feel like I'm going to vomit from the smell and I sense the presence linger a moment, stare at me perhaps, and then say, "Your cup will be here waiting for you."

They disembark and the doors shut very quickly.

I stay in the elevator. It pauses, waiting for input. If I strain, I think I can hear the bass of the song and then some kind of toast.

Then the elevator descends to the ground floor and the sound falls away. The doors open to a plain, concrete maintenance hall. The same level as from the start.

I stare at the empty walls ahead.

Did that really just happen? Perplexed. And I think, no, it didn't. It couldn't have. If I go back up there, it's going to be empty just like before, just as it was the first fifteen or twenty times I went up. But I'm a little scared this time. *Your cup will be here waiting for you.* Will a group of people greet me when I get up there, like a surprise birthday party? Me with feigned shock, and everyone clapping like the end of *Evangelion. Congratulations!* they'll all say, *you made it! You're alive!* Yes. That's exactly what it is. It has to be.

I look at the silver panel of cab controls, scornful. Apprehensive, I press ten. The doors close and I travel up.

O NLY I NEVER MAKE it there. Caustic soda party or not, on ten, the elevator brakes hard and jerks against the cables. The lights snap off and I'm engulfed in black. I clutch onto the wall like a mantis, and the cab shudders, buoys for a second, then stops.

Words crawl across the floor indicator panel in red LED, one letter at a time.

ACCESS DENIED: BY INVITATION ONLY!

Huh. Didn't realize a Kool-Aid party was such a highfalutin affair. I watch the letters march across the screen a moment and a voice comes on over the elevator intercom.

"*Name?*"

"What—? Hello?"

"*Name?*" With a little more impatience this time. The irritated cadence of a clerk at a vehicle registration counter.

"I'm trying to get to ten."

"*I can see that.* Name?"

"Vicken."

"*Vicken what?*"

"Asatryan."

"*I don't see you on the list.*"

"List? S-sorry, I'm a little lost?"

"*Uh-huh. If you're a plus one, you have to arrive on time. If you don't arrive on time you're not allowed in. We're very punctual at our events here.*"

"Where is *here* exactly?"

"*The Tenth Floor.*"

"Ah. Well, if you won't let me in, can you let me out?"

"*Whatever do you mean?*"

"To an exit. Outside. 'Cause I can barely fucking breathe in here and I haven't seen the sun shine in God-knows-how-long."

"*If you want to file a complaint, you have to go to sublevel six on the B-wing and fill out the pink and blue forms.*"

"I'm good. No complaints. I just want to get *out*."

"*Well, that's accessible on Ground.*"

I press G for Ground. Nothing.

"It's busted. It won't even light."

"*What won't light?*"

"G. Ground. The button."

"*The elevator button?*"

What fucking else?

"Yes."

"*Oh.*"

"Oh?"

An extended pause. The crackle of radio waves shimmers over silence.

"*I'm going to have to transfer your call to Maintenance for that.*"

"Oh my fucking God." The words spill out of me. "*Just open the goddamn door!*"

But the intercom clicks off and I'm met with a quiet that stretches long.

And then the emergency lights tinker to life, but we're not moving.

Just fucking peachy.

I hit the alarm button and it blares a brief *bzzz*. Silence.

I depress the buttons for all the floors, mash the maintenance button repeatedly.

Nothing.

I'm going to be fucking stuck—

"*Thank you for calling Maintenance.*"

My head snaps up.

"*In response to the increased volume of calls due to the number of safety issues related to a sense of helplessness, we've created a dedicated hotline to issues related to crises. For claustrophobic issues, please press 1. If pain is a lyric your body has composed, please press 2. If you want to do it right this time, press 3. If you have taken the elevator to reminisce, please press 4. For all other issues, please remain on the line.*"

"Hello?"

A long pause, followed by: "*… Please remain on the line while we reroute your call to the nearest technician in our network.*" And then, "*Hello?*"

Holy shit. "Is someone there?"

"*Hello?*"

"Wha— can you hear me? I'm stuck."

"*I can hear you just fine, sir. No need to yell.*"

"Okay. God, sorry. It's been a minute since I've…" I bark out a little staccato laugh and rake a hand through my hair. "I'm stuck. I'm stuck in an elevator."

"*Do remain calm.*"

"I am calm. I'm not budging."

"*Do move to the rear of the elevator because emergency services may attempt to open the door.*"

I move as far back as I can.

"Yeah. Done."

"*Don't try to exit and don't panic. Don't attempt to pry open the doors.*"

"I haven't attempted anything."

"*What is your emergency?*"

Dizzying verbal dance, my answers coming round again like a bolero. "I told you. I'm trapped. Crammed in a box dangling from a piano wire."

"*What is the name of the building where the elevator is located?*"

I lean back against the cool steel wall, racking my mind for clues. Nothing special about this place. All landmarks reduced; slow-motion shades of grey. "I don't have an answer. I honest to God don't know where I am."

"*Okay. This is what we'll do and then we can talk about it: I*" *need you to take a step back from the situation. Breathe deep, so you don't act impulsively.*

"*It's okay to have a little trouble. Sometimes these machines need some oiling; that's what Maintenance is here for.*" Faint keyboard clatter as she logs the information. "*Are you injured?*"

"—in the elevator?" Shame tongues at my skin. "Like from an accident?"

"*No, from the incident.*"

"… what incident?"

"*The one on file.*"

"It—what? Can you just call a repairman? Or a firefighter or something?"

"*If you need to talk about something, we can talk.*"

"I don't need to talk; I need to get the fuck out of here! I'm fucking suffocating. I want to get out of here."

"*I'm not a machine, sir.*"

"I know that. Christ."

"*I know that you're upset but you need to be civil. If you can't, then I'm going to have to close this line.*"

"The fuck? You're not supposed to do that!"

Silence.

"—hello?"

"*Are you going to be civil?*"

"Stop treating me like I'm a fucking child!"

"*Okay. Have a good day. Goodbye.*"

"Wait. Wait!"

I batter my finger against the call button like it's an old controller. I feel like I'm talking to the fucking *Alice in Wonderland* doorknob. I'm at my fucking limit.

A line of static, then the same intro note as before, followed by a deep breath, an exasperated sigh. The voice, which should ground me, does nothing but reinforce at a distance my solitude.

"*We're here to help as many people as possible, sir.*"

"I know that. I'm sorry. Please help me," I bleat desperately.

Silence.

"Please. I'm sorry. I just need help."

"*Okay, give me a minute. How would you like me to assist? Where would you like to go?*"

"What? Anywhere. Out."

"*Out?*"

"Yeah. Like, home, I guess."

I've said the words before I can understand them. *Home.* My sacred centre of the world.

"*Home?*"

"Yeah. Home."

"*Home,*" the voice says. She types this into her computer. "*What was home like?*"

A library. Soft seasons. Yes, but also: a place where I returned after indescribable loss, where I took the most psychic pain, a place where things got broken and repaired, and rearranged.

Could it be both?

She speaks to me like a mother. She tells me: *why not?*

God, because the wicked truth of it was that home was a horrible loneliness. Despite the spectacle of house parties and sweet-scented oleander blossoms gifted with feigned sympathy, home was a trap. A grey vault to lock away my animal body. Home was where the dark came early, stayed, draped heavy like a blanket over me when I slept, and nightmares rearranged the furniture with every season so that I felt further from the fireplace, the window, and an empty doorway, which seemed too far to cross. I was there but no one I really wanted came to see me. How could I feast on such memories? How could I call such squalor home?

"Was that what it really was?"

I fall quiet and think it over. The difference between what I want home to be and what home was. Trying to get a grip on what the fuck home took the shape of and before I know it, I'm spewing a long line of incoherent sentences.

Something about it has moved. Is moving. Has there ever been a place I called home? There was Armenia, and then Versailles (less decadent than the history books), then Montreal (more racist than the history books). But when I think about what home truly was, the weight of reality seems downright Sisyphean. Home was the kaleidoscopic strain of my mother rooming in my shitty apartment—the one that constantly dripped a single pearl of cold water in an otherwise lukewarm shower-head; the one that smelled of black mould; the one where she was always wrist-deep in my business—and when it wasn't that, it was my cat, Pickles, ripping to shreds my greedily lent pile of secondhand books, and if it wasn't that, it was my mom's sleep apnea, and her snoring that kept me awake so often I chose to instead take night-shifts in the ambulance so I could sleep in the day. Maybe if I'd been a doctor and not a paramedic, I could've prescribed myself some sleep medications. Home? Was home where I should bring a date, thirty-two and living with my mom? No. Home was not the little sanctuary where I could bring boys, the handsome ones I sometimes dreamed I'd come across, chasing the sun west on their roadster, my arms tight around their waist, the thick, syrupy smell of leather there to whisk me off to sleep as I lay my head down on their shoulder for a rest.

No. Home, much like this place, had no extraneous ornaments, no decorative flares to look at. It was a dark, quiet room to *suffer* and *exist*, built of an architectural language of industrialization and aggressive brutishness. Home was big, brutish, foreign. Lonely. Like me.

That's what it was.

But that's not what I say.

Instead, what I finally say is something I don't believe.

"Someone who loves me."

I can almost feel her smile.

"I think I can do that. Okay. Are you ready? Press the Maintenance button, and think of home."

I feel like an idiot, for certain, but I press the button and try to picture home. Picture him. Felix, even. His arms. There is a desperate effort not to think of these other things, but all the good things fade away and home is reduced to noise. A single, thunderous noise.

Then something happens. Top to bottom, all the lights start to flicker on and off in sequence like a Broadway marquee. The floor display above the doors flickers a mash of numbers and then counts down from ten. Once the clock hits zero, it flashes red and the Maintenance button shocks my fingertip with a white-hot singe.

"What the hell!"

I stagger back.

"*Our time is up. Your service is complete,*" the Maintenance clerk chimes.

I brace myself against the back wall handle. I begin to feel faint, and a sense of falling, like something's sucked all the air out of me. My vision gyres and I lower myself to the ground, the aperture of the world closing in on me fast. A strong somnolence possesses me. The sound of her voice vanishes in the solitude.

"*Thank you for calling Maintenance,*" the clerk says. "*I hope you find your way home.*"

The grey falls away and it all goes dark.

THE END

If you're reading this, I'm dead.

Haha, sike. Just kidding. Gotcha.

No. Regrettably, I'm still here. Sifting through memories in delirium, miserable in the impervious grey house in the cold. The elevator has sunk me deeper, because apparently there's floors below the ones listed on here.

Waking up to be coughed back out on some new territory. When it brackets its doors behind me with a sigh, it shudders out a death rattle and they don't open again after that.

New floor this time, oh goodie.

Frosted glass door, like a hospital or a Belgian spa. Pushing past and on my way across the room on hands and knees. Tired. How many ways can the body be tired?

What hits me first is the odour of decay, rancid and cloying. Death and flowers, blood and bone. I squeeze my eyes shut and the flint-quick flash of the lampricide footage strobes behind my eyelids.

There's an unhewn gravel feel against my hands, so I drag my palm across the floor experimentally. It's all been mixes of gunmetal grey until this point (and sometimes, when it's feeling generous, a bit of rusted red), but this is something else. I smooth my fingertips across the topography. It comes away, granulated sand-like grit, and when I open my eyes again I can see, not sand, but the shelled carapaces of dead insects: thousands of them—amphimallons and curled moth larvae, pupae skins, and moulted cuticles—all crushed beneath me. I sit back on my heels. Pulpy excreta stick to my palms and I wipe them off on my pant legs and finally get a good look at the room.

The whole thing gives me pause.

A monumental atrium with astonishing volume, it's much larger than many of the other rooms. A soaring ceiling fifty feet up slants off like an orthogonal mine, dimming the room cavernous. Its roof is a cracked dome, ribbed like twist-ties and stained with brown grime as though it had been unearthed at some point. Fluorescent lights glower in dim, thin shafts. It stains the atmosphere, colours the walls with an anemic complexion. Up there, almost impossible to see—a flutter of movement chandeliers over me: winged insects drunkenly swarming against the dusty, dirty acrylic light diffusers, covered in grime. They pelt themselves against the forever daylight of this place, then drop their wings, soon to die.

The room is wide as it is long, the size of a throne room, though devoid of any brocade-decadence, or baroque ornamentation, its walls plain, water-stained concrete.

At the centre of the room, breaking the monotony of the expansive floors, is something holy: a baptismal font, but enormous—this tranquil body of water, the size of a small lake, rippled by the eddy of some unseen breath. Its earthy blue-green colour is a shock in the world of oppressive grey.

I advance. Around its edge, moss and reeds sprout from cracks in the foundation. And closer, flowers: crested iris and wild geraniums, all up, holding their heads high and spreading their petals towards a simulated sun. I feel I am like them too: touch-starved and deprived of warmth.

The pool they surround might very well be a well of embittered tears. Tears of sorrow and grief, courage and endurance. How fitting it would be, then, for me to drown in a pit of them: drift down like a night spectre into the heart of it and find forever stillness there. The only home that I can ever have. The only one I've ever known. The thought makes me ill.

Perhaps it's pumped in water from who-knows-where—a tributary of the Saint Lawrence River, maybe; wouldn't that be fitting? Funny.

Heh. Fuck. On the ground, knees drawn up to my chin. I can feel my depression closing in on me. I want to absolve myself of the violence of this, splicing myself between hope and despair. But it feels like a prophecy and the thought of that unmoors something in me. The providence of exactly what I came here to do meeting me in the middle, this ugly decision, and by this, I feel, in my body, like the sudden cold spot of a haunted manor. It seeps across the cracked leather of my skin. A wound that bleeds me, erodes me. A perfumed strip of Papier d'Arménie torn from a booklet, alight, that dances, sears and curls until it is reduced to ash. Do I know why I want to die? Those reasons seem empty. What extremely personal tragic event in a person's life should make it so that a man might take his own life? It's hard to tell if these things matter or not. Why are you vultures all circling me like you need a clue? Sometimes it's grueling and pointless and you want out, so you do. *Point final.* It's pretty explicit.

Anyway, a moment like this is impossible to overlook. I've tried other things, but there's no other option. After everything, this is all there is.

There's no point in checking the enclaves of other halls. This room is the one.

This is what it is. Murky water and crests of dirt under the nails, and rocks in the pockets.

I don't want to be alone for this, but I guess you're here. And it's not so bad in this room. It's quiet. It'll be better like this.

Hurry, hurry.

Last time, when I called the hotline they'd just said get yourself as far away from the thing as possible. You're so tired from it all that reaching up over the top of the fridge is too much effort to grab the knife so you don't even do it. That's why antidepressants have the black box label. They don't make you want to kill yourself; they just give you enough energy to finally move on it. And it might seem as though a great appetite has risen in me for it, but make no mistake: I am only tired.

I stand up and then I'm grabbing handfuls of rocks—insect carapaces catching, wriggling between my fingers—and just dumping them into the pockets of my coat, my pants. They weigh down on my meagre findings—Felix's subway ticket and the Coin Eye Skeleton's coins and my empty tackle box—until my pockets are comically full.

And then I wade in, and it's freezing like the Saint Lawrence would be this time of year. The water slows me. My movements are sluggish, and I, a pebble on this wondrous lake, make ripples against her mirrored face, sinking deeper and deeper—

Before taking a sure step forward off the shelf break to submerge completely into the drop-off. I want to feel relief, but its edges are singed with despair—

And there, reality erodes.

I tip through the jaws of dark matter, tumbling through into a great black nothingness, devoured into the belly of the beast. Inside: a vast, comfortless cosmic void. The water here is so cold. Trying to forget. Trying to release the air in my lungs, if only I could. With all this cement in me, my body feels so heavy. I'm sinking right down, no pocket pebbles needed.

The water is losing its icy touch. It's kind of nice: suspended up on a cloud, poised against the stars. I wish I could drift in it like this forever. If death is like this—one long kiss with slumber—it will be nice. I think about this and I close my eyes. No more maudlin goodbyes. I lower myself into that silent urn, and drown.

I CAN SEE THE FLOWERS growing around the base of the lake, bowing over the face of the water, constellations of indigo petals falling above me. Trailing along like sylvan clouds. I read faces, shapes, and animals out of the patterns. That's called pareidolia. Like gentle foam. All of it, so beautiful.

If the choice is mine, I know which one to make.

I don't quite know why, but I think I might want to stay.

THE FLOWERS ARE SO beautiful, but I can't have regrets, you know? In a minute, these things won't matter to me. All the rest of this will just be blank empty pages. One great, big ellipsis.

A LAPSE IN JUDGEMENT.

There's something down here with me.

The inky concrete basin unfurls in murky angles. In the pit of it, invisible to me from the surface, are columns of those fused-together bodies, half-stripped of skin, their emptied husks vaguely visible from the dark. Yearning to add nodules to their bulk.

And me, staring back mutely at these inhuman replicas, watching as I watch, sinking ever closer in the dark down there, dim and cold, and damp—not their eyes but their grasping hands reaching up to me, dribbles of dark ichor ribboning out their mouths—and I feel a dread so palpable, so full, so absolute, that the pressure of it all crystallizes in me a single capricious thought singing with a resonance I've never known:

No.

My resolve breaks like waves on a cliff. Carapaces that form an enormous concretion in my pockets, monstrously heavy, sink me down into this astral stomach like a stone, towards that star-white pyre of bodies blazing against the oppressive blackness.

As I sink closer, a clutch fruits off of the bowels of the filth, laboriously wiggling up through the cavernous depths. Cat's cradle of flesh and bone stretch and unream, severed heads rolling over the dunes of itself, delicate and elongating, and *hungry* to ascend like a bloated fish gaping on a beach, their sickening faces bobbing up through the blackness towards me in frantic haste. Their frozen dead eyes, terrifying like the face of a Babylonian god.

And it jousts me with panic like a cattle prod. I'm all animal fear—do animals fear God?—and my hands are battering against the heavy rocks in my pockets, casting them out like sins. Praying my body: be kinder, be lighter. I commit myself to life; I commit myself to colour.

Kicking up lake sediment, churning the water with clouds of silt so I can't see anything, I can't fucking see them anymore, but I can *feel* them snapping at my heels with clawed hands. I know they're just behind me, close enough that if I don't kick to swim for shore, for my fucking *life*, I know where I'll end up.

Another doughy bloated corpse, digested by time, like that woman's waterlogged remains in the rooftop cistern, drowned and decomposing inside the glutted belly of a colony a hollow mile beneath the surface of the Earth—it's almost got me; I can feel a spindly hand grip round my ankle and I'm thrashing hard against it, thinking, *No, no, no*.

Out of air, out of air, can't breathe like this, dumping rocks, just dumping, can't look down with that split-second adrenaline *PANIC* etching lightning channels through my arteries, lungs burning—

And suddenly I'm breaking the event horizon of the water's surface.

I come up gasping for air.

Scrambling, kicking and flailing and choking. Grasping and ripping, uprooting the irises growing at the bank. All of the rocks and shit come tumbling out of my pockets, and I clamber through wreckage, coughing up spittle and river water until it feels like there's nothing left.

I dribble my soaking body out onto the charcoal-grey shore, and I think I've pissed myself, at least I'm pretty sure I have. Dotting the dry concrete wet, backing away, my palms smacking against the ground. A new life birthed by the uterine waters of this river body. A remission of my sins. A baptism. A second life, though it doesn't feel like a gift.

The skin where it had touched me is raw and blistering, cyanotic. An almost welcome pain after stretches of numbness. A crushed, milky pus emits from my pores and eats away at my pant leg, so I yank it up.

The proof is there, burrowing fissures into my muscle. It looks like a long tapeworm pressed up and around my instep, turning the tissue there grey.

I leach out a whine. I don't want to touch it. I keep cutting between looking at it—wriggling under my skin—and staring at the surface of the water. I'm just waiting for particles of it to charge the air, floating up like ash, and for their gurgling screams as they puncture the face of the water.

Only they don't.

It takes a couple of minutes of me sucking in sharp gulps of breath like a fish on the wharf before I realize nothing's coming out of there. Nothing is chasing me.

I try to stand, and my strength exhumes from me like an ebbing tide. Adrenaline's all gone now and I can't help but stumble drunkenly out a doorway at the back of the room. Can't remember if it was there before, but beyond it's another hallway, big surprise, and that just siphons the rest of my energy totally out. My calves are aching knots, and my chest floods heavy. I drag my wet body to a corner away from the lake room and collapse somewhere near a wall. I look down at myself—my hands are shaking—and I worry, and I worry. This place could be a hundred-thousand square kilometres, infinitely growing like stars moving apart in space and I might never reach the end. Borges' Library of Babel, void of books. But what can I do? What can I do?

The maelstrom of noise inside my head continues for so long, my exhaustion and fragility begin to put me to sleep in spite of it all and when I do fall asleep, I do so all at once. Like holding back the dawn, it cannot be dampered.

M AYBE I'M A LITTLE high from chugging river water; maybe I'm tired of taking my own bad advice. Either way, you know what? Fuck this. I'm tired. Jesus, take the wheel. Treat this like a coin flip, or, if you want, like a video game. What should I do next?

If I find my way out and have a nice dinner date with Felix,
turn to page 112.

If I lie down on the ground and seep through the floor like
muck, my eyes dribbling into ribbons of fluid paste out my orbital
bones and I come to be part of the network of red weed bodies
trapped here forever, turn to page 111.

If you let me decide what to do, turn to page 119.

YOU'D LIKE THAT, WOULDN'T you? You like making people miserable? You like seeing people make themselves miserable? I bet you went to Rotten dot com as a kid. You're a perverted jackass who should have your head examined. You're the type to watch animals corralled in a zoo enclosure, flinging shit at each other, screeching when kids flare at them, mistaking their fear response for excitement. Newsflash, asshole: it's not excitement; it's a deep-down primordial fear. Is that what you want? You want to see me scared; you want to see me squirm? Fine. Here it goes: I lie down on the ground and seep into a paste, my soul bound to a starless underground chasm and all that's left of me is a fat dark cum stain on the earth of this place like a ghost out of *Pulse*. There. Is that what you wanted? Does that make you happy, you sick fuck?

If it does make you happy (and you know it) clap your hands.

And/or otherwise, turn to page 121.

THAT'S NICE OF YOU. Life just turns around and goes really fucking well for me all of a sudden, huh? Okay. So, I find a glowing exit blinking like a neon sign at a sex club. I travel on through and there's a nice speakeasy on the other side, some sultry buxom blonde with legs to her tits draining torch songs onstage, and Felix is by the bar waiting for me. And we sit and he buys me a drink, and when I go to the bathroom he follows, because I'm so beautiful, who can resist; I've been a charmer my whole life and the whole room's got eyes on me—the whole world, even. He kisses me with such tenderness, it tastes of wine and rose and salt ecstasies, and I think I know for an instant what it's like when Dante wrote in such sacred poem that love is God, that the force of love is a temple that could move both sun and stars, a home to call our own. He sucks me off in the bathroom with a greed I didn't even know possible, and I have the most earth-shattering orgasm. Stars explode behind my eyes and God himself comes down and gives me a high five. It truly doesn't get any better than this! And then I wake up and I'm still in this shithole of a subway station, abandoned fifty thousand feet below ground because this is all a dream—it's not possible for me to leave this place, don't you get it, asshole?—and now you've made me cream my pants from a wet dream and I've got no change of clothes so I'm gonna be stuck with crusty briefs for the rest of my short, shitty existence, so thanks for that.

If you offer me a change of clothes, turn to page 114.

If you want to hear a joke, since you're such a chucklefuck, turn to page 115.

T HANKS, ASSHOLE. REAL NICE of you.

If you want a formal apology, turn to page 118.

S O THERE'S THIS MAN—he's from Bulgaria, or wherever—and he loves trains. Like, fucking *loves* trains. The guy's been obsessed with them, dreaming of driving one since he was a kid, spends his whole life thinking about this one singular fucking thing like it's God's gift to us all. Obviously, when he's old enough, he applies to work for a railway. That shit gets denied, but the obsession's still there, so he's like, *fuck it*, and I guess his fixation gets the better of him because one day he just hijacks a train.

Mind you, despite being obsessed with 'em, the guy knows nothing about trains, or maybe it's just this specific train; all he knows is, he wants to go *fast*.

So he does—*choo-choo*—goes real fast, passengers and all—and he's so stoked, he gets a little reckless, and, well, the whole thing ends in a big fucking crash. Just the worst.

He makes it out all right, though. A little scratched up, but he's good. Then again, someone else dies, so the train guy's arrested.

He goes to court and *boom*, our little rail fan's found guilty, and he's sentenced to death.

When the day of his execution comes, they do the thing they always do, which is ask inmates what they want their last meal to be. And the guy just says, "A single banana."

Easy enough.

Guy gets his fix, quick word from our sponsor, the priest, then they strap him to a chair and give him the old sparky.

Sparks fly, smoke fills the air, but the guy doesn't die. In fact, our guy's totally fine.

Of course, the executioner's baffled; he's never seen anything like this, not in his twenty-six years on payroll, and no one really knows what else to do, 'cause *technically* he's served his sentence. And you can't punish a man twice for the same crime, so they just let him go.

Within a week, the guy (who's obsessed with trains), naturally, goes and steals another one. Doesn't care that he can't drive them, doesn't care that the last run ended in a catastrophe, just *fucking loves trains.*

As before, our man crashes it. As before, he's sentenced to stand trial. Shows no remorse, only extreme delight in driving trains, and is again sentenced to death.

And you better believe the request for his last meal's a single banana.

When he goes to ride the lightning, the executioner pulls the switch but nothing happens. Well at this point, shit, this must be an act of God. And the law hasn't changed since the last time; they gotta let him go, so again, they do.

So this train-obsessed maniac, again on the loose, does what any sensible man would do. He wastes no time; he hijacks another train. Of course, crashes it.

His trial is quick, 'cause they're familiar with this guy at this point, and he's again sentenced to death. Day of his reckoning, asked what he wants for his last meal and again he says:

"A single banana."

Okay, well now the executioner's pissed, he's been through this charade twice already, so he's like, "No you fucking don't, you son of a bitch, we're onto you with this whole stupid banana trick! You're not getting away with it this time!"

And they don't let him pick a meal, they just feed him a steak and buttered toast.

The next morning they strap him into the chair, flip the switch and… nothing happens.

"What the fuck!" says the head guard. "Did you give him the banana?"

"No, sir!" says the guard. "Didn't give him a thing, we swear!"

Turns out the banana had nothing to do with it. He was just a really bad conductor.

Turn to page 121.

I CAN'T DO THIS ANYMORE. I just want to lie down and die.

Sorry, there's supposed to be a page turn here. Just flip it, I'm sure whatever's next is fine.

Turn to page 121.

YOU WANT ME TO choose? Me? What gives you the right? I told you I don't want to be here anymore. Isn't it obvious? Isn't it all so glaringly fucking obvious? You want me to choose? You want me to choose love? Just tell me what you want. Use the words. Tell me what you want to see; I'll say and do whatever you want me to do. Why? Why do you care? You can't change how it ends. The story's in your hands. No, it's *literally in your hands*. When this thing gets published, my ending will already have been written. You choosing and me choosing doesn't change a goddamn thing.

So, let's… just… agree not to choose, yeah? It's kinda nice here, right? Nothing sinister. We've got a *Monster at the End of the Book* thing going on and if you just drop it here, neither of us has to be my antagonist and see what it is. *They Both Die at the End*, and *John Dies at the End*—perhaps I should just name this thing *Maybe I Die at the End!*—denial's as good a drug as any.

You and I both know, the longer I stay here, the more I fall into stasis. Petrified like fossilized driftwood. So don't paginate any further, and we can pretend like I've always just been here riding these halls, because I'm pretty sure I have; it's been like this in my life longer than it hasn't. We can leave it written as it is, like this:

Dear Diary,

Yesterday and today have been bad days

But tomorrow, I still hope.

And I can wrap those words round my neck like a noose and choke on them.

Turn to page 121.

DOWN A FEW MORE empty halls, back, somehow, near the sets of metaled teeth that first spit me out into this place, I'm punctured by a sound—not of a train—but of the distant call of a payphone. And with that, I've discovered a goal.

Takes me a minute, but I find my way around to the source, and by the time I do, the phone stops ringing and doesn't start up again. I think, *Please, God, let me not have discarded the coins in that feral race to remove rocks from my pockets.* I fish through them and out they tumble onto my shaking palm: two coins, round and silver, perfectly alike. There's also the wet subway ticket with Felix's number on it adhering to my skin. The concrete there is fading to calluses, lighter, maybe, etched with new palmistry lines of raised scars.

I'd almost forgotten about the ticket. I lift the receiver to my ear and the dial tone hits. Drop in a coin and then… nothing, 'cause my head's gone blank. I've never had anyone to call. This is exactly why I'd called the hotline before, again and again. It's not healthy to put your well-being in someone else's hands. That's what I'd always told myself, but there's a balance and I'd tipped the scales in the wrong direction, made an island of myself to the point where even the sun and stars looked foreign to me, a satellite planet in isolation. Even Pluto has Charon to dance with.

Have you ever thought to put your life in God's hands? Is it really so far-fetched to believe he might care? Isn't that what's so appealing about religion? That God believes in you. That the universe is always conspiring to grant your life its colour. That everything's meant to lead you not only up to this point, but further, so that you can see exactly how far it is you've come.

I press the heels of my palms over my eyes. I don't know what to do here.

I plead with myself. Let me have this one thing and then I can go. There's no one. Alone. Alone. Alone. There's no right answer. Only,

If I call Felix, turn to page 123.

If I call home, turn to page 128.

If I press *69 to return the call, turn to page 130.

I DROP IN A COIN and dial the number from the ticket. Immediately, like histamines released from itching a scab, I want to hang up. The feeling flares even more strongly when I hear a voice on the other end.

"Hello?" he says.

"Hey."

Silence. Maybe he doesn't remember me. Hesitation. How long has it even been? The self-destructive impulse to slam down the receiver detonates in my head.

"Do you recognize my voice?" I ask.

"Vicken, from the subway."

"Yeah."

"Yeah, hey. I remember. How was the beach?"

I scoff out a laugh. "I didn't go."

"Yeah? Thought it was kind of weird someone would go this late in the season, but didn't want to press about it. You sound kind of far away."

"I'm calling from a payphone. Are you real?"

"What? Are you wasted? You calling for a ride or something?"

"God, no," I answer. "I don't even know how you'd get to where I am to pick me up."

"What did you get yourself into? Did you fall through a

toilet into Narnia?"

"I'm—I have no idea." I laugh.

"When are you coming back?"

"Can't really say. I don't know that I can come back."

"What do you mean? How'd you get there?"

"I took the Metro."

"Just take the same way back."

"It's not that simple."

"Cryptic. Just grab a ticket, hop the line, *bing-bang-boom*."

The absurd simplicity of it all makes me feel so stupid. If only it were that simple. God. I'm laughing again. Maybe it is.

"What if I don't have a ticket?"

"I mean, I wrote my number on one. How else would you be calling? You memorize it or something? 'Cause if you did, that's a pretty astronomical red flag."

I turn it over in my hands, its satin gloss making it impermeable to the river water. I grin sheepishly.

"So you did."

"It still had some fares, in case you were wondering the cost of that thirst."

"Consider the debt repaid, what with me calling from a payphone and everything."

He chuckles. "Okay. When you find your way back, wanna meet up at a bar?"

Ah, *fuck*. If this is a dream and I wake up again with cum stains on my junk, I'm going to be so fucking pissed.

"No," I say, a little too quick.

"Oh?"

"No—" I make a small sound. "I mean. Someplace else. In daylight. I do still want to see that exhibit."

"I think it's done."

"Oh…"

"We'll figure something out."

There's a where and when. I tell him not to hold it against me if I don't show up.

It is this tiny kindness, this little extension of grace, that holds me for a time after I hang up. Talking to him—Felix—glitter blown from the palm. My sojourn here feels so insurmountably large; exhausting; an impotence that gnaws at me like a cancer, still, but—there's a sprout blooming in the desert. Vivid green after so many months of grey. A colour away from the stillness. Its fragrance filled with a headiness that feeds the stars, blows out the sky, doesn't belong here, not in a place so dark, a subterranean world so grey and lifeless. I want to write myself out of here, so I will.

There is a heaven in being near things you know. I consider it a prayer.

My eyelids are heavy. Somewhere between waking and dream, the lights churn, hypnotic. I may have one coin left but I don't need it.

Turn to page 126.

AFTER EVERYTHING, I SUPPOSE I must concede defeat. I am a failed suicide. Lying on a park bench, on a deliciously warm day for Montreal, I try to live again.

Slowly, colour uncurls its delicate sleeping form. Sunlight combs its teeth through fields of chartreuse grass, as tiny winged creatures tremble out the golden mouths of flowers. To my right, a queer couple, deliriously in love, lay their bodies entwined on a milky-pink linen blanket, as they paint dragons and sailboats of fair-weather clouds. Beyond, on the pier, a woman with a white lace parasol twirls it in the sun. Further yet, that same sun reddens the waves of the Saint Lawrence River, rushing softly to break against the shore.

I can see myself going to that grey tomb once more. There's no avoiding going back there, but I still love this place, I think— enough to make me want to stay. I do my part to mitigate my suffering by admitting a dangerous and painful love. My heart opens to it like rain clouds: the love of adventure, of men, of pleasure. The sun and the wild geranium meadows, good epigraphs, and the beautiful songs of Arvo Pärt, and dazzling laughter, and the deep earth power of soil between my toes, and talks in the twilight hour, sax buskers, and the taste of wine, the burning heat of love, and naps and dreaming. Replete is the body which holds for us these sublime ecstasies, replete with sanctity and graces, all of it so briefly; it glitters wondrously on the ground, then extinguishes like a flame. I feel the blood rush of affection for it, protective, to cradle it like a small animal, a child.

The sun's rays needle my skin. Soft petals of wind braid hope through my hair. I tilt my head back for a sip of water, and then I open my eyes.

And there he is: a small miracle.

His steeped earthen hair, his eyes, soft brown, as telescopes that spot a blooming nebula across the night sky. Dressed in striking white, his silhouette blots out the sun. He smiles. The height of tenderness in his eyes is enough to make me melt.

All of it is still bleached. Desaturated. There is no vibrant hue until his lips on mine, a most bruising kiss, and a burst of colours whirls behind my eyelids, caramelized by the tongue of a small god of mercy. My body thrums, an aubade. Having been awakened, I reach up towards my lover, as he gently holds me by supporting my head and chest. *Psyche Revived by Cupid's Kiss.* How calm, how still this makes me. Rapturous. The kiss of lips, and not: the waves. How it shakes me with furious hope.

The End

R ING…
    Ring…

Ring…

No one picks up.

I have one coin left. Who else should I call?

If I call Felix, turn to page 123.

If I call home again, turn to page 129.

If I press *69 to return the original missed call, turn to page 130.

THE MOST BITTERSWEET CONSOLATION. It goes to voicemail. Of course it does. Who's going to pick up—me?

Beeeeep.

What would you say if you could talk to your younger self? What I want to say is, *Your life sucked yesterday, it sucks today, it's going to suck tomorrow. We've been here before and we'll be here again.* Sometimes I can barely even remember the in-betweens, the other stations, the warm air of outside. Winter seems to drag for so long, it feels like stasis doesn't differ from death, but if it's enough to know that all storms must have their season, a time to plant, and a time to cull, and that if you want change, that wanting's half the battle, then it's up to you.

I stare out from a station isolated from all the world and wonder if I can return from such a distant atmosphere without burning on re-entry. I might. I might not.

Words of affirmation have always been my chosen love language.

"You're doing great," I say. And I hang up the phone.

Relapse to page 23.

H ERE COMES THE FINAL, unholy communion.

Full disclosure: I know this conversation. It didn't happen so long ago. It's my voice. Like I'm picking up a line, eavesdropping on an old recording. I remember I couldn't cry. The feeling was there, just the tears wouldn't come. But hearing myself again, now, they fall.

"What have you done? Be clear with me, Vicken. Do I need to call someone?" The suicide hotline rep. Word of advice: don't ever call those places. Oh, you'll step back from the precipice all right, but it won't be because you want to. They just wear you down. Talk it over until you're deflated of impulse.

"No. No, don't call anyone." I can hear the embarrassment in my voice. It's shaking.

I remember thinking I shouldn't have ever called anyone. Especially not a hotline. Forget what I said before—who can you call when you've got no one? I won't make the same mistake twice. The world's meant to be experienced with others; what makes a beach is the collective grains of sand.

"Promise me you'll call back." I can't make that promise. It's funny now, though; in retrospect, I guess I have. Like listening to a tape-recorded message of myself, I feel like I'm reaching through time. "Vicken, promise me you'll call back or I'll send someone."

"I'm gonna miss some of this shit. That's the worst part, I'm going to miss it."

"Why don't you wait until tomorrow?"

"I've been waiting. I've waited. I can't anymore."

There's some amnesia around this. I barely remember what comes next, only that I woke up in the hospital after three days. A trail mix of tangerine and powder-blue pills. Popping 'em back like M&M Minis. My mom was the only one who was there. She stayed up all night, because you just don't know. After this, I spent four days at the Douglas Mental Health University Institute, almost pissing myself in fear. When I was there, I really got to think about it—it'd been incubating in me for longer than I realized. Here, too, it does. It's just—it's exhausting. It feels bottomless. Recursive. I don't think anything has really changed, give or take a few years. Same endless droll of grating self-awareness. Whatever—you picked this—that's on you. It's not like I fucking knew.

It's not like I wanted to mess with you, have that revelation all on our own—and yeah, here we are, just listening to my endless sniveling, selfish navel-gazing—I hate it, you know, some parts were unexpected, the beginning was nice, and the part in the middle with the elevator was fun, but this is just too much. It seems almost insincere, hiding between the pages of an openness that's just—

For the longest time, this felt like an inevitability. When I was eighteen, I couldn't see myself living to thirty-two. Now that I'm thirty-two, I can't see myself living to sixty. I just can't. I feel like I'm headed for an early retirement. Nothing seems scarier to me than that. My body becoming my prison, a petrified man, pinned by life's Medusa gaze. People always baulked when I told them I didn't want kids. What for? *Well, who's going to take care of you when you're old?*—that's always the first thing they say is, *Who's gonna take care of you when you're old?* What, like having kids is a guarantee they're going to love you enough to want to care for you, bathe you, clothe you, wipe your diapered ass as you did theirs, knowing damn well they're on a one-way track careening towards the same inevitable fate, just give it another twenty-five, thirty years? Kids or no kids, loneliness lives in our bodies more than ourselves. The signs of it are everywhere for me, cross-hatched Jacob's ladders trammeled along the crook of my elbow. At one point, I stopped having enough shame to hide it on my lower half. Everyone has too much pity to ask, nobody wants to take the time, and those that do, do so in their own self-interest. The only time anyone ever said anything was an ex, on our way hiking when in the striking heat I was wearing shorts in his car, and he stroked his thumb along my thigh while he was driving (something I always thought was so intimate), tracing the topography of white and raised scars that lived there, and simply remarked, reducing an entire lifetime of suffering—every single instance that drew me to hate myself enough to carve those channels in my skin to begin with, over and over again, for years on end, well into my twenties, relapsing more often than I can count—to three little words:

"I've seen worse."

That gave me enough fuel for a few weeks of therapy, and anyway, I don't know why I'm thinking of it here. There's kind of a demented mirth that takes over me, now that I've made my decision. I hang up the phone and I kind of wish I'd taken your advice back there and done what you'd told me to do. I'm laughing; it's that strange, elated sort of grief that follows life's sometimes maddening karmic justice.

Working my way backwards like a dungeon crawl, speedrunning suicide, *Look, Ma, here I go for the world record!* until I find the swamp room again—or lake, I guess. Takes me a while to get there, the mission of it becoming a project that demands all my focus. No more eating, no more rests. No piss breaks. I stumble along like a wounded animal in a terrible wind. And when I find it, I punch a hole through the glass window in the door—it takes a couple times, because it's small, rectangular, firm, like trying to break an egg from the top instead of the middle—and when it shatters against my fist and dark rivulets of blood come bubbling out, it feels *good*.

I grab a piece of glass—the biggest I can find, like a long, sharp blade—and hold it in my palm as I wade into the water and—

Sometimes I think when it happens, I'll fade into sadness, sadness, such incredible sadness, but what it really is is exhaustion, and anger. I'm so fucking tired. Everything I've ever loved about life has been robbed from me, and there's no moment of respite that'll make it any better.

And—oh, the only thing I wish about it right now is that I hadn't lost so many weeks to it, so many weeks, like mementos to moves, I wish I'd gone a little crazy at the end, I wish I hadn't wasted… but, you know, capitalism's got its fucking death grip around us all, I couldn't even—can you imagine? Can you fucking imagine? If I'd drained it all—every penny I had saved up for an apartment—on an extravagant trip to France, I could've even brought someone with me—I wonder if anyone would've even accepted the generosity—but, and—is it really me then? Is it really me doing this? I can't, fuck, man, this gets your head all up in a loop. Words are sluggish, tongue heavy, reality's edges loosening. The tide inside me surging, surging. It doesn't matter. What I'm trying to say is, if none of that other stuff was in place, maybe I would've stayed. You ever think about that? How fucking much, exactly, is lost to that? It doesn't matter. I'm tired. I've never been so tired. I cradle my head, and this time I do it, I let go. I have to have this feverishness in me to go. I can't do it otherwise. It's—it is a vicious thing, it is. It really is. My body's so weakened, now. So frail. Death, fraying away at my edges, threatening to sink me into an insensate middle age. The faint revulsion of my own body. Thin breath, acid stomach, limbs tapered as when I was a child. To prevent it from spoiling, I stab hard and fast across my jugular. My throat clenches with a fury. I begin to scream and vibrate. Goddamn, look at me go.

Are you seeing this? Jesus fucking Christ, I think I'm drowning in it. There *is* colour in this place, there *is*, the small red cherry of it, flaming up, turning the grey walls incarnadined.

I slash away at that fucker with everything I've got in me like I'm trying to cut straight through to the spine, like I'll come out the other end in a paper blue sky.

Gurgling, choking against water, bubbles—

No more! No more, no place where I end and the rest of it begins—

And the theatrics of it all! Stop me if I begin to pontificate but I've been practically sleepwalking through life; I've barely seen anyone here, not a single soul besides Pashmina, and it's not like I would look favourably upon them if I did, so it's nice to have someone to narrate this to, to witness me lay hands upon myself—

And if it's not me, it's someone else. There are a million ways in which the body is stolen from us—debt and interest and data and labour and literal tissue and blood that can be harvested, and affective, sexual, and emotional energy. Capitalists, which clutch and pry and feed, dreaming up ways in which they can make your body not your own, and when the last drop of blood is exhausted they'll have the audacity to bill you for it. Bodies are the crude oil of the economy, and what do you do with crude oil? You extract and deplete it.

And when I do finally do it—drag the sharp edge of it across my skin, deeper than I've ever gone before, and drown into and under the water, I think how pathetic this is. What a comedy of errors. How barbarous, how demented, how awful. Maybe it's not. I can't decide if what I am doing is a brave and dignified truth, a love letter of sorts, or if it is sad and cowardly. But it's too late now. None of this is enough to keep me.

Much later, as long as you'd like for that to be, when all the kudzu has claimed the buildings back and the satellites complete their lifetime and burn up in the atmosphere, the lake of that place will have drained, and on the ground, like some strangely anthropomorphic pillar, you'll find my body. I'm dissolved, like Pashmina, like rare pearls in wine—or, dissolved isn't the right word. From mid-cheek down, I am a pottery clay statue that looks like it's taken to flame, blisters of refracted anatomy cutting up out of me at odd angles like pillars of bismuth crystal. Patches of powdery white mycelium travel up my arms, my torso, rooted to the ground. My skin is thinning so much, like from radiation poisoning, that veins are visible. My entrails are beginning to slip out the thinness of my skin. They pool at the base of me, like the cooled wax of a melted candle. I am paved into the floor; trapped in a cage of flesh. A prison of stone. And from the looks of it, I'm quite alive.

THE END

ACKNOWLEDGEMENTS

FIRST AND FOREMOST, I'D like to thank my editor, Daniel Carpenter. His tremendous faith and careful eye on every detail of this project, both large and small, is the thoughtful and devoted work every writer dreams of working with. I'm forever grateful.

Thanks to those who read early drafts and offered insight and invaluable friendship: M. Lopes da Silva, Adrian Leigh, Scott J. Moses (my day one—I knew when Scott liked this book that I had written something to be proud of).

Thank you to Jess Landry, the very first person to read my work and find something special in me. She helped make me the writer I am today.

To the collective of talented artists who endorsed this book, many amongst whom I'm overjoyed to call close friends—I am humbled and thankful for the support lent to this project.

My deep, abiding gratitude to Chad Luibl for his generosity and profound sincerity.

A special thanks to Chris McAllister, the immensely creative mind behind our gorgeously evocative book trailer. Thank you to the gracious team at Titan for their help in bringing this book to readers—Bahar, Izzy, Katharine. Natasha, thank you for your affecting cover art.

Thank you to Lucia Peters for sharing translated information on 'The Elevator Game'. Her chilling handbook *Dangerous Games to Play in the Dark* has many more dark and delicious games to play.

Thank you to my parents. To Isa, my familiar.

My heartfelt thanks to my friends and writing group coconspirators: Lyndsie Alguire, Andrew F. Sullivan, Christi Nogle, Shelley Lavigne, J.A.W. McCarthy, Angela Sylvaine, Alexis Dubon, Tiffany Michelle Brown, Carolee Flatley, Kathe Koja, Jonathan Louis Duckworth, Sapphire Lazuli, Rae Wilde, and Evelyn Freeling.

A debt of gratitude to Cassandra Khaw for their erudition, guidance and friendship during this strange and wonderful journey.

And, of course, my greatest thanks to Len. My safe harbour, my storybook ending. The center of my world, whose love buoyed me through the writing of this book. Every moment, every choice, was a butterfly effect that led me to you. You are the greatest gift of my life.

And thanks to you, reader, for enduring the ugliness and loveliness that limn the pages of this book. Your life matters. Thanks for reading to the very end.

ABOUT THE AUTHOR

SOFIA AJRAM IS A metalsmith, writer and editor who specializes in feverish stories of anomalous architecture and queer pining. He is the editor of *Bury Your Gays: An Anthology of Tragic Queer Horror*. She has also given lectures on contemporary horror films at Monstrum Montreal and serves as a moderator of r/horror on Reddit. Sofia lives in Montreal with her cat Isa.

sofiaajram.com
X: @sofiaajram
TikTok: @sofiaajram
Instagram: @sofiaajram
Bluesky: @sofiaajram

For more fantastic fiction, author events,
exclusive excerpts, competitions, limited editions and more

VISIT OUR WEBSITE
titanbooks.com

LIKE US ON FACEBOOK
facebook.com/titanbooks

FOLLOW US ON TWITTER AND INSTAGRAM
@TitanBooks

EMAIL US
readerfeedback@titanemail.com

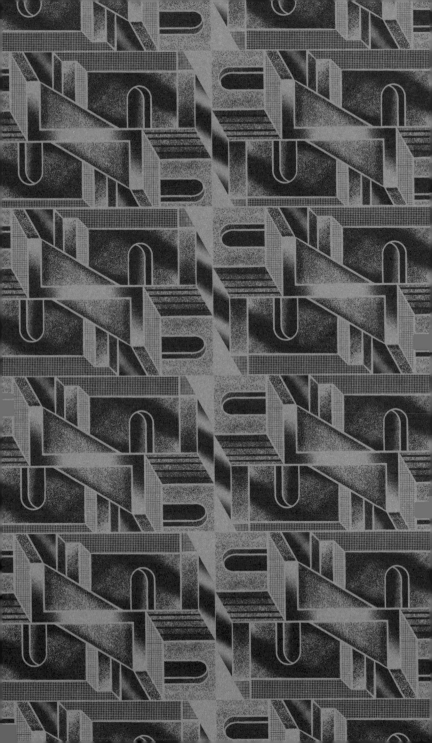